WANKH

Originally titled *Servants of the Wankh*, [illegible] of Jack Vance's most famous series, th[illegible] of Adventure tetralogy. This classic SF novel continues the adventure of Adam Reith, an Earthman marooned on an alien planet and facing constant danger as he struggles to steal a spaceship from the deadly Wankh. In the planet Tschai, Jack Vance has created an exotic world as fully realized as Dune or Barsoom.

JACK VANCE

The only author to have won the Hugo, the Nebula, and the Edgar Awards, Jack Vance has written dozens of novels of science fiction, fantasy, and mystery. His recent works include *The Green Pearl, Lyonesse, Rhialto the Marvellous,* and *Cugel's Saga*. In addition to the Planet of Adventure series, his most famous works are *The Dying Earth, The Languages of Pao,* and the Demon Princes series.

PHILIP HAGOPIAN

He is a young artist whose debut as a book illustrator came with Bluejay's edition of *Rogue Queen* by L. Sprague de Camp. He is illustrating all four of the Planet of Adventure series. He lives in West Danville, Vermont.

BLUEJAY ILLUSTRATED EDITIONS

Great works of imaginative fiction illustrated by top artists, Bluejay Illustrated Editions are a continuing series of books that include the works of writers such as Mildred Downey Broxon, L. Sprague de Camp, Theodore Sturgeon and Jack Williamson, and artists such as Tom Kidd, David G. Klein, Rowena Morrill, and Timothy Kirk. All are printed on acid-free paper and sturdily bound in handsome trade paperback format with heavy cover stock.

Jack Vance's

Planet of Adventure Tetralogy

Tschai I: Chasch

Tschai II: Wankh

*Tschai III: Dirdir

*Tschai IV: Pnume

*forthcoming

TSCHAI II

WANKH

By

Jack Vance

BLUEJAY BOOKS INC.

A Bluejay Book, published by arrangement with Tor Books

Book design by Joann Willig

Manufactured in the United States of America

First Bluejay printing: April 1986

This book is printed on acid-free paper. The paper in this book meets the guidelines for permanence and durability of the Committee on Production Guidelines for Book Longevity of the Council on Library Resources.

Library of Congress Cataloging in Publication Data

TSCHAI II

WANKH

PRELIMINARY

TWO HUNDRED AND TWELVE LIGHT-YEARS FROM EARTH HUNG THE smoky yellow star Carina 4269 and its single planet Tschai. Coming to investigate a mysterious surge of radio signals, the survey ship *Explorator IV* met destruction. The sole survivor, star-scout Adam Reith, was rescued, barely alive, by Traz Onmale, boy-chief of the Emblem nomads.

From the first, Adam Reith's urgent goal was to return to Earth, with news of Tschai and its queer conglomerate of peoples. In his quest for a suitable spaceship he was joined by Traz, then by one Ankhe at afram Anacho, a fugitive Dirdirman.

Tschai, so Reith learned, had been the scene of ancient wars between three off-world races: the Dirdir, the Chasch, and the Wankh. An uneasy stalemate now existed, each race maintaining an area of influence, with the vast hinterlands abandoned to nomads, fugitives, bandits, feudal lords, and a few more or less civilized communities. Indigenous to Tschai were the solitary Phung and the Pnume, a furtive race occupying caverns, tunnels, and passages under the ruined cities which marked the Tschai landscape.

Each of the alien races had indentured or enslaved men who across thousands of years had evolved toward the host race, so that now there were Dirdirmen, Chaschmen, Wankhmen, and Pnumekin, in addition to other, more obviously human peoples.

From the first Reith had marveled at the presence of men on Tschai. One evening at a Dead Steppe caravansary the Dirdirman Anacho clarified the matter: 'Before the Chasch came, the Pnume ruled everywhere. They lived in villages of little domes, but all traces of these are gone. Now they keep to caves and dark fastnesses, and their lives are a mystery. Even the Dirdir consider it bad luck to molest a Pnume.'

'The Chasch came to Tschai before the Dirdir?'' Reith asked.

'This is well-known,' said Anacho, wondering at Reith's ignorance. 'The first invaders were Old Chasch, a hundred thousand years ago. Ten thousand years later the Blue Chasch arrived, from a planet colonized an era earlier by Chasch spacefarers. The two Chasch races fought for Tschai, and brought in Green Chasch for shock troops.

'Sixty thousand years ago the Dirdir appeared in force. The Chasch suffered great losses until the Dirdir arrived in large numbers and themselves became vulnerable, whereupon a stalemate went into effect. The races are still enemies, with little traffic between them.

'Comparatively recently, ten thousand years ago, space-war broke out between the Dirdir and the Wankh, and extended to Tschai when the Wankh built forts on Rakh and South Kachan. Now there is little fighting, other than skirmishes and ambushes. Each race fears the other and bides its time. The Pnume are neutral and take no part in the wars, though they watch all with interest and make memoirs for their great history.'

'What of man?' Reith asked guardedly. 'When did they arrive on Tschai?'

'Men originated,' said the Dirdirman in his most didactic manner, 'on Sibol and came to Tschai with the Dirdir. Men are as plastic as wax. Some metamorphosed, first into marshmen, then, twenty thousand years ago, into his sort.' Here Anacho indicated Traz, who glowered back. 'Others, enslaved, became Chaschmen, Pnumekin, even Wankhmen. There are dozens of hybrids and freakish races. Variety exists even among the Dirdirmen. The Immaculates, for instance, are almost pure Dirdir. Others exhibit less refinement. This is the background for my own disaffection: I demanded prerogatives which were denied me but which I adopted in any event . . .'

Anacho spoke on, describing his difficulties, but Reith's attention wandered. It was now clear how men had come to Tschai. The Dirdir had known space-travel for more than seventy thousand years. During this time they had evidently visited Earth, twice at the very least. On the first occasion they had captured a tribe of proto-Mongoloids—the apparent nature of the marshmen to which

Anacho had alluded. On the second occasion—twenty thousand years ago, according to Anacho—they had collected a cargo of proto-Caucasoids. These two groups, under the special conditions of Tschai, had mutated, specialized, re-mutated, re-specialized to produce the bewildering complexity of human types now to be found on the planet.

Accompanying the caravan across the Dead Steppe were three Priestesses of the Female Mystery and their captive: the Flower of Cath, to use her formal name, or Ylin Ylan, her flower name, or Derl, her friend name. She was a girl of remarkable beauty, of medium height, exquisitely formed if rather slight, with dark shoulder-length hair, a complexion like thick cream. Her face in repose was apt to be pensive, even melancholy, as if her adventures had given her cause for gloom, as well they might. At first glimpse Reith had been fascinated; at the second he had become entranced. He took the girl under his protection and promised to see her safely home.

From Cath, he now learned, had originated the radio signals which had attracted the *Explorator IV* to Tschai. Torpedoes had devastated the Cath cities Settra and Ballisidre, apparently in response to the radio signals. A torpedo had destroyed the *Explorator IV*. Who had launched the torpedoes: what people, what race? No one knew.

At Cath Reith hoped to find the facilities to construct a small spaceboat. Obtaining a sky-raft at Pera, the City of Lost Souls, Reith set out to the east, accompanied by Traz, Anacho the Dirdirman, and the Flower of Cath.

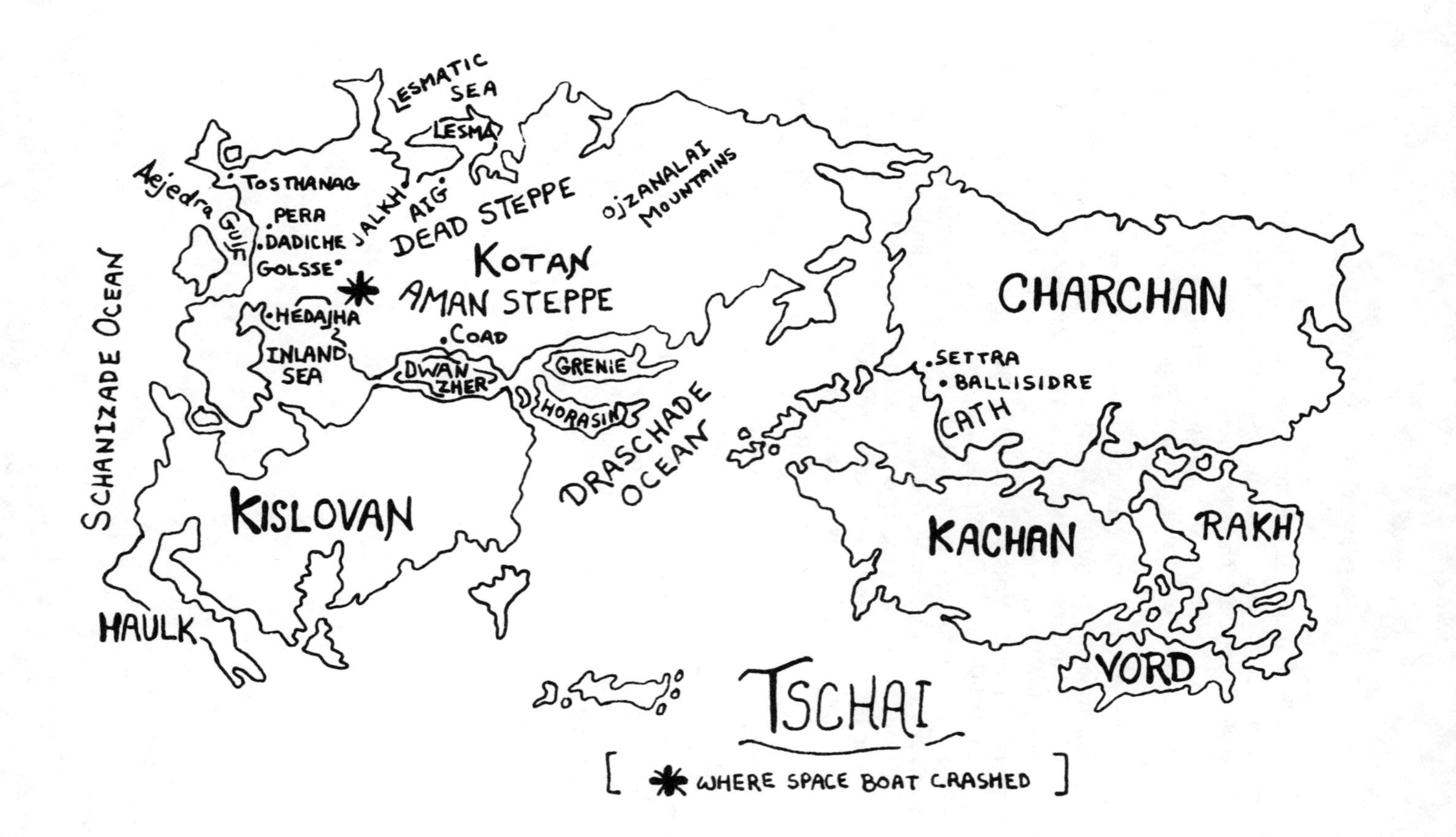
Lesmatic Sea
Lesma
Aejedra Gulf
Tosthanag
Pera
Dadiche
Golsse
Jalkh
Aig
Dead Steppe
Ojzanalai Mountains
Kotan
Aman Steppe
Hedajha
Coad
Inland Sea
Dwan Zher
Grenie
Horasin
Draschade Ocean
Schanizade Ocean
Kislovan
Haulk
Charchan
Settra
Ballisidre
Cath
Kachan
Rakh
Vord
TSCHAI
[✱ WHERE SPACE BOAT CRASHED]

I

TWO THOUSAND MILES EAST OF PERA, OVER THE HEART OF THE Dead Steppe, the sky-raft faltered, flew smoothly for a moment, then jerked and bucked in a most ominous fashion. Adam Reith looked aft in dismay, then ran to the control belvedere. Lifting the voluted bronze housing, he peered here and there among the scrolls, floral hatchings, grinning imp faces, which almost mischievously camouflaged the engine.* He was joined by the Dirdirman Ankhe at afram Anacho.

Reith asked, "Do you know what's wrong?"

Anacho pinched up his pale nostrils, muttered something about an "antiquated Chasch farrago" and "insane expedition to begin with." Reith, accustomed to the Dirdirman's foibles, realized that he was too vain to admit ignorance, too disdainful to avow knowledge so crass.

The raft shuddered again. Simultaneously from a four-pronged case of black wood to the side of the engine com-

*Such elaborations were neither ornament nor functional disguise, but expressed, rather, the Chasch obsession for complication as an end in itself. Even the nomadic Green Chasch shared the trait. Examining their saddlery and weapons, Reith had been struck by a similarity to the metalwork of the ancient Seyths.

partment came small rasping noises. Anacho gave it a lordly rap with his knuckles. The groaning and shuddering ceased. "Corrosion," said Anacho. "Electromorphic action across a hundred years or longer. I believe this to be a copy of the unsuccessful Heizakim Bursa, which the Dirdir abandoned two hundred years ago."

"Can we make repairs?"

"How should I know such things? I would hardly dare touch it."

They stood listening. The engine sighed on without further pause. At last Reith lowered the housing. The two returned forward.

Traz lay curled on a settee after standing a night watch. On the green crush-cushioned seat under the ornate bow lantern sat the Flower of Cath, one leg tucked beneath the other, head on her forearms, staring eastward toward Cath. So had she huddled for hours, hair blowing in the wind, speaking no word to anyone. Reith found her conduct perplexing. At Pera she had yearned for Cath; she could talk of nothing else but the ease and grace of Blue Jade Palace, of her father's gratitude if Reith would only bring her home. She had described wonderful balls, extravaganzas, waterparties, masques according to the turn of the "round." ("Round?" What did she mean by "round?" asked Reith. Ylin Ylan, the Flower of Cath, laughed excitedly. "It's just the way things are, and how they become! Everybody must know and the clever ones anticipate; that's why they're clever! It's all such fun!") Now that the journey to Cath was actually underway the Flower's mood had altered. She had become pensive, remote, and evaded all questions as to the source of her abstraction. Reith shrugged and turned away. Their intimacy was at an end: all for the best, or so he told himself. Still, the question nagged at him: why? His purpose in flying to Cath was twofold: first, to fulfill his promise to the girl; secondly, to find, or so he hoped, a technical basis to permit the construction of a spaceboat, no matter how small or crude. If he could rely

P.W.HAGOPIAN©86

upon the cooperation of the Blue Jade Lord, so much the better. Indeed, such sponsorship was a necessity.

The route to Cath lay across the Dead Steppe, south under the Ojzanalai Mountains, northeast along the Lok Lu Steppe, across the Zhaarken or the Wild Waste, over Achenkin Strait to the city Nerv, then south down the coast of Charchan to Cath. For the raft to fail at any stage of the journey short of Nerv meant disaster. As if to emphasize the point, the raft gave a single small jerk, then once more flew smoothly.

The day passed. Below rolled the Dead Steppe, dun and gray in the wan light of Carina 4269. At sunset they crossed the great Yatl River and all night flew under the pink moon Az and the blue moon Braz. In the morning low hills showed to the north, which ultimately would swell and thrust high to become the Ojzanalais.

At midmorning they landed at a small lake to refill water tanks. Traz was uneasy. "Green Chasch are near." He pointed to a forest a mile south. "They hide there, watching us."

Before the tanks were full, a band of forty Green Chasch on leap-horses lunged from the forest. Ylin Ylan was perversely slow in boarding the raft. Reith hustled her aboard; Anacho thrust over the lift-arm—perhaps too hurriedly. The engine sputtered; the raft pitched and lurched.

Reith ran aft, flung up the housing, pounded the black case. The sputtering stopped; the raft lifted only yards ahead of the bounding warriors and their ten-foot swords. The leap-horses slid to a halt, the warriors aimed catapults and the air streamed with long iron bolts. But the raft was five hundred feet high; one or two of the bolts bumped into the hull at the height of their trajectory and fell away.

The raft, shuddering spasmodically, moved off to the east. The Green Chasch set off in pursuit; the raft, sputtering, pitching, yawing, and occasionally dropping its bow in a sickening fashion gradually left them behind.

The motion became intolerable. Reith jarred the black case

again and again without significant effect. "We've got to make repairs," he told Anacho.

"We can try. First we must land."

"On the steppe? With the Green Chasch behind us?"

"We can't stay aloft."

Traz pointed north, to a spine of hills terminating in a set of isolated buttes. "Best that we land on one of those flat-topped peaks."

Anacho nudged the raft around to the north, provoking an even more alarming wobble; the bow began to gyrate like an eccentric toy.

"Hang on!" Reith cried out.

"I doubt if we can reach that first hill," muttered Anacho.

"Try for the next one!" yelled Traz. Reith saw that the second of the buttes, with sheer vertical walls, was clearly superior to the first—if the raft would stay in the air so long.

Anacho cut speed to a mere drift. The raft wallowed across the intervening space to the second butte, and grounded. The absence of motion was like silence after noise.

The travelers descended from the raft, muscles stiff from tension. Reith looked around the horizon in disgust: hard to imagine a more desolate spot than this, four hundred feet above the center of the Dead Steppe. So much for his hope of an easy passage to Cath.

Traz, going to the edge of the butte, peered over the cliff. "We may not even be able to get down."

The survival kit which Reith had salvaged from the wrecked scout boat included a pellet gun, an energy cell, an electronic telescope, a knife, antiseptics, a mirror, a thousand feet of strong cord. "We can get down," said Reith. "I'd prefer to fly." He turned to Anacho, who stood glumly considering the sky-raft. "Do you think we can make repairs?"

Anacho rubbed his long white hands together in distaste. "You must realize that I have no such training in these matters."

"Show me what's wrong," said Reith. "I can probably fix it."

Anacho's droll face grew even longer. Reith was the living refutation of his most cherished axioms. According to orthodox Dirdir doctrine Dirdir and Dirdirmen had evolved together in a primeval egg on the Dirdir homeworld Sibol; the only true men were Dirdirmen; all others, were freaks. Anacho found it hard to reconcile Reith's competence with his preconceptions, and his attitude was a curious composite of envious disapproval, grudging admiration, unwilling loyalty. Now, rather than allow Reith to excel him in yet another aspect, he hurried to the stern of the sky-raft and thrust his long pale clown's face under the housing.

The surface of the butte was scoured clean of vegetation, with here and there little channels half-full of coarse sand. Ylin Ylan wandered moodily across the butte. She wore the gray steppe-dwellers' trousers and blouse, with a black velvet vest; her black slippers were probably the first to walk the rough gray rock, thought Reith. . . . Traz stood looking to the west. Reith joined him at the edge of the butte. He studied the dismal steppe, but saw nothing.

"The Green Chasch," said Traz. "They know we're here."

Reith once more scanned the steppe, from low black hills in the north to the haze of the south. He could see no flicker of movement, no plume of dust. He brought out his scanscope, a binocular photo-multiplier, and probed the gray-brown murk. Presently he saw bounding black specks, like fleas. "They're out there, for a fact."

Traz nodded without great interest. Reith grinned, amused as always by the boy's somber wisdom. He went to the sky-raft. "How go the repairs?"

Anacho's response was an irritated motion of arms and shoulders. "Look for yourself."

Reith came forward, peered down at the black case, which Anacho had opened, to reveal an intricacy of small components. "Corrosion and sheer age are at fault," said Anacho.

"I hope to introduce new metal here and here." He pointed. "It is a notable problem without tools and proper facilities."

"We won't leave tonight then?"

"Perhaps by tomorrow noon."

Reith walked around the periphery of the butte, a distance of three or four hundred yards, and was somewhat reassured. Everywhere the walls were vertical, with fins of rock at the base creating crevices and grottos. There seemed no easy method to scale the walls, and he doubted if the Green Chasch would go to vast trouble for the trivial pleasure of slaughtering a few men.

The old brown sun hung low in the west; the shadows of Reith and Traz and Ylin Ylan stretched long across the top of the butte. The girl turned away from her contemplation of the east. She watched Traz and Reith for a moment, then slowly, almost reluctantly, crossed the sandstone surface and joined them. "What are you looking at?"

Reith pointed. The Green Chasch on their leap-horses were visible now to the naked eye: dark motes hopping and bounding in bone-jarring leaps.

Ylin Ylan drew her breath. "Are they coming for us?"

"I imagine so."

"Can we fight them off? What of our weapons?"

"We have sandblasts* on the raft. If they climbed the cliffs after dark they might do some damage. During daylight we don't need to worry."

Ylin Ylan's lips quivered. She spoke in an almost inaudible voice. "If ever I return to Cath, I will hide in the farthest grotto of the Blue Jade Garden and never again appear. If ever I return."

Reith put his arm around her waist; she was stiff and unyielding. "Of course you'll return, and pick up your life where it left off."

*Sandblast: a weapon electrostatically charging and accelerating grains of sand to near-light speed, with consequent gain in mass and inertia. Upon penetrating a target, the energy is yielded in the form of an explosion.

"No. Someone else may be Flower of Cath; she is welcome. . . . So long as she chooses other than Ylin Ylan for her bouquet."

The girl's pessimism puzzled Reith. Her previous trials she had borne with stoicism; now, with fair prospects of returning home, she had become morose. Reith heaved a deep sigh and turned away.

The Green Chasch were no more than a mile distant. Reith and Traz drew back to attract no notice in the event that the Chasch were unaware of their presence. The hope was soon dispelled. The Green Chasch bounded up to the base of the butte, then, dismounting from their horses, stood looking up the cliff face. Reith, peering over the side, counted forty of the creatures. They were seven and eight feet tall, massive and thick-limbed, with pangolin-scales of metallic green. Under the jut of their crania their faces were small, and, to Reith's eyes, like the magnified visages of feral insects. They wore leather aprons and shoulder harness; their weapons were sword which, like all the swords of Tschai, seemed long and unwieldy, and these, eight and ten feet long, even more so. Some of them armed their catapults; Reith ducked back to avoid the flight of bolts. He looked around the butte for boulders to drop over the side, but found none.

Certain of the Chasch rode around the butte, examining the walls. Traz ran around the periphery, keeping watch.

All returned to the main group, where they muttered and grumbled together. Reith thought that they showed no great zest for the business of scaling the wall. Setting up camp, they tethered their leap-horses, thrust chunks of a dark sticky substance into the pale maws. They built three fires, over which they boiled chunks of the same substance they had fed the leap-horses, and at last hulking down into toad-shaped mounds, joylessly devoured the contents of their cauldrons. The sun dimmed behind the western haze and disappeared. Umber twilight fell over the steppe. Anacho came away from the raft and peered down at the Green Chasch. "Lesser

Zants,'' he pronounced. ''Notice the protuberances to each side of the head? They are thus distinguished from the Great Zants and other hordes. These are of no great consequence.''

''They look consequential enough to me,'' said Reith.

Traz made a sudden motion, pointed. In one of the crevices, between two vanes of rock, stood a tall dark shadow. ''Phung!''

Reith looked through the scanscope and saw the shadow to be a Phung indeed. From where it had come he could not guess.

It was over eight feet in height, in its soft black hat and black cloak, like a giant grasshopper in magisterial vestments.

Reith studied the face, watching the slow working of chitinous plates around the blunt lower section of the face. It watched the Green Chasch with brooding detachment, though they crouched over their pots not ten yards away.

''A mad thing,'' whispered Traz, his eyes glittering. ''Look, now it plays tricks!''

The Phung reached down its long thin arms, raised a small boulder which it heaved high into the air. The rock dropped among the Chasch, falling squarely upon a hulking back.

The Green Chasch sprang up, to glare toward the top of the butte. The Phung stood quietly, lost among the shadows. The Chasch which had been struck lay flat on its face, making convulsive swimming motions with arms and legs.

The Phung craftily lifted another great rock, once more heaved it high, but this time the Chasch saw the movement. Venting squeals of fury they seized their swords and flung themselves forward. The Phung took a stately step aside, then leaping in a great flutter of cloak snatched a sword, which it wielded as if it were a toothpick, hacking, dancing, whirling, cutting wildly, apparently without aim or direction. The Chasch scattered; some lay on the ground, and the Phung jumped here and there, slashing and slicing without discrimination the Green Chasch, the fire, the air, like a mechanical toy running out of control.

Crouching and shifting, the Green Chasch hulked forward. They chopped, cut; the Phung threw away the sword as if it were hot, and was hacked into pieces. The head spun off the torso, landed on the ground ten feet from one of the fires, with the soft black hat still in place. Reith watched it through the scanscope. The head seemed conscious, untroubled. The eyes watched the fire; the mouth parts worked slowly.

"It will live for days, until it dries out," said Traz huskily. "Gradually it will go stiff."

The Chasch paid the creature no further heed, but at once made ready their leap-horses. They loaded their gear and five minutes later had trooped off into the darkness. The head of the Phung mused upon the play of the flames.

For a period the men squatted by the edge of the precipice, looking across the steppe. Traz and Anacho fell into an argument regarding the nature of the Phung, Traz declaring them to be products of unnatural union between Pnumekin and the corpses of Pnume. "The seed waxes in the decay like a barkworm, and finally breaks out through the skin as a young Phung, not greatly different from a bald night-hound."

"Sheer idiocy, lad!" said Anacho with easy condescension. "They surely breed like Pnume: a startling process in itself, if what I hear is correct."

Traz, no less proud than the Dirdirman, became taut. "How do you speak with such assurance? Have you observed the process? Have you seen a Phung with others, or guarding a cub?" He lowered his lip in a sneer. "No! They go singly, too mad to breed!"

Anacho made a finger-fluttering gesture of fastidious didacticism. "Rarely are Pnume seen in groups; rarely do we see a Pnume alone, for that matter. Yet they flourish in their peculiar fashion. Brash generalizations are suspect. The truth is that after many long years on Tschai we still know little of either Phung or Pnume."

Traz gave an inarticulate growl, too wise not to concede the conviction of Anacho's logic, too proud to abandon

P.W. HAGOPIAN©86

abjectly his point of view. And Anacho, in his turn, made no attempt to push a superficial advantage home. In time, thought Reith, the two might even learn to respect each other.

In the morning Anacho again tinkered with the engine, while the others shivered in the cold airs seeping down from the north. Traz gloomily predicted rain, and presently a high overcast began to form, and fog eased over the tops of the hills to the north.

Anacho finally threw down the tools in boredom and disgust. "I have done what I can. The raft will fly, but not far."

"How far, in your opinion?" asked Reith, aware that Ylin Ylan had turned to listen. "To Cath?"

Anacho flapped up his hands, fluttering his fingers in an unknowable Dirdir gesticulation. "To Cath, by your projected route: impossible. The engine is falling to dust."

Ylin Ylan looked away, studied her clenched hands.

"Flying south, we might reach Coad on the Dwan Zher," Anacho went on, "and there take passage across the Draschade. Such a route is longer and slower—but conceivably we will arrive in Cath."

"It seems that we have no choice," said Reith.

II

FOR A PERIOD THEY FOLLOWED THE SOUTHWARD COURSE OF THE vast Nabiga River, traveling only a few feet above the surface, where the repulsion plates suffered the least strain. The Nabiga swept off to the west, demarcating the Dead Steppe from the Aman Steppe, and the raft continued south across an inhospitable region of dim forests, bogs, and morasses; and a day later returned to the steppe. On one occasion they saw a caravan in the distance: a line of high-wheeled carts and trundling house-wagons; another time they came upon a band of nomads wearing red feather fetishes on their shoulders, who bounded frantically across the steppe to intercept them, and were only gradually outdistanced.

Late in the afternoon, they painfully climbed above a huddle of brown and black hills. The raft jerked and yawed; the black case emitted ominous rasping sounds. Reith flew low, sometimes brushing through the tops of black tree-ferns. Sliding across the ridge of the raft blundered at head-height through an encampment of capering creatures in voluminous white robes, apparently men. They dodged and fell to the ground, then screaming in outrage fired muskets after the raft, the erratic course of which presented a shifting target.

All night they flew over dense forest, and morning revealed more of the same: a black, green, and brown carpet cloaking the Aman Steppe to the limit of vision, though Traz declared the steppe ended at the hills, that below them now was the Great Daduz Forest. Anacho condescendingly took issue, and displaying a chart tapped various topographic indications with his long white finger to prove his point.

Traz's square face became stubborn and sullen. "This is Great Daduz Forest; twice when I carried Onmale among the Emblems,* I led the tribe here for herbs and dyes."

Anacho put away the chart. "It is all one," he remarked. "Steppe or forest, it must be traversed." At a sound from the engine he looked critically aft. "I believe that we will reach the outskirts of Coad, not a mile farther, and when we raise the housing we shall find only a heap of rust."

"But we will reach Coad?" Ylin Ylan asked in a colorless voice.

"So I believe. Only two hundred miles remain."

Ylin Ylan seemed momentarily cheerful. "How different than before," she said, "when I came to Coad a captive of the priestesses!" The thought seemed to depress her and once more she became pensive.

Night approached. Coad still lay a hundred miles distant. The forest had thinned to a stand of immense black and gold trees, with intervening areas of turf, on which grazed squat six-legged beasts, bristling with bony tusks and horns. Landing for the night was hardly feasible and Reith did not care to arrive at Coad until morning, in which opinion Anacho concurred. They halted the motion of the raft, tied to the top of a tree and hovered on the repulsors through the night.

After the evening meal the Flower of Cath went to her

*The Emblems: nomads setting great store by small fetishes of metal, wood and stone, each with a name, history, and personality. The warrior wearing a particular emblem becomes imbued with its essence, and in effect becomes the emblem. Traz carried Onmale, the paramount emblem of the tribe, and so was the ritual chief.

cabin behind the saloon; Traz, after studying the sky and listening to the sounds of beasts below, wrapped himself in his robe and stretched out on one of the settees.

Reith leaned against the rail watching the pink moon Az reach the zenith just as the blue moon Braz rose behind the foilage of a far tall tree.

Anacho came to join him. "So then, what are your thoughts as to the morrow?"

"I know nothing of Coad. I suppose we inquire as to transportation across the Draschade."

"You still intend to accompany the woman to Cath?"

"Certainly," said Reith, mildly surprised.

Anacho hissed through his teeth. "You need only put the Cathwoman on a ship; you need not go yourself."

"True. But I don't care to remain in Coad."

"Why not? It is a city which even Dirdirmen visit from time to time. If you have money anything is for sale in Coad."

"A spaceship?"

"Hardly. . . . It seems that you persist in your obsession."

Reith laughed. "Call it whatever you like."

"I admit to perplexity," Anacho went on. "The likeliest explanation, and one which I urge you to accept, is that you are amnesiac, and have subconsciously fabricated a fable to account for your own existence. Which of course you fervently believe to be true."

"Reasonable," Reith agreed.

"One or two odd circumstances remain," Anacho continued thoughtfully. "The remarkable devices you carry: your electronic telescope, your energy-weapon, other oddments. I cannot identify the workmanship, though it is equivalent to that of good Dirdir equipment. I suppose it to be home-planet Wankh; am I correct?"

"As an amnesiac, how would I know?"

Anacho gave a wry chuckle. "And you still intend to go to Cath?"

"Of course. What about you?"

Anacho shrugged. "One place is as good as another, from my point of view. But I doubt if you realize what awaits you in Cath."

"I know nothing of Cath," said Reith, "other than what I have heard. The people are apparently civilized."

Anacho gave a patronizing shrug. "They are Yao: a fervent race addicted to ritual and extravaganza, prone to excesses of temperament. You may find the intricacies of Cath society difficult to cope with."

Reith frowned. "I hope it won't be necessary. The girl has vouched for her father's gratitude, which should simplify matters."

"Formally the gratitude will exist. I am sure of this."

" 'Formally?' Not actually?"

"The fact that you and the girl have formed an erotic accommodation is of course a complication."

Reith smiled sourly. "The 'erotic accommodation' has long since run its course." He looked back toward the deckhouse. "Frankly, I don't understand the girl. She actually seems disturbed by the prospect of returning home."

Anacho peered through the dark. "Are you so naïve? Clearly she dreads the moment when she must sponsor the three of us before the society of Cath. She would be overjoyed if you sent her home alone."

Reith gave a bitter laugh. "At Pera she sang a different tune. She begged that we return to Cath."

"Then the possibility was remote. Now she must deal with reality."

"But this is absurdity! Traz is as he is. You are a Dirdirman, for which you are not to blame—"

"No difficulties in either of these cases," stated the Dirdirman with an elegant flourish of the fingers. "Our roles are immutable. Your case is different; and it might be best for all if you sent the girl home on a cog."

Reith stood looking out over the sea of moonlit treetops.

The opinion, assuming its validity, was far from lucid, and also presented a dilemma. To avoid Cath was to relinquish his best possibility of building a spaceboat. The only alternative then would be to steal a spaceship, from the Dirdir, or Wankh, or, least appealing of all, from the Blue Chasch: all in all, a nerve-tingling prospect. Reith asked, "Why should I be less acceptable than you or Traz? Because of the 'erotic accommodation?' "

"Naturally not. The Yao concern themselves with systematics rather than deeds. I am surprised to find you so undiscerning."

"Blame it on my amnesia," said Reith.

Anacho shrugged. "In the first place—possibly due to your 'amnesia'—you have no quality, no role, no place in the Cath 'round.' As a nondescript, you constitute a distraction, a zizyl-beast in a ballroom. Secondly, and more poignant, is your point of view, which is not fashionable in contemporary Cath."

"By this you mean my 'obsession?' "

"Unfortunately," said Anacho, "it is similar to an hysteria which distinguished a previous cycle of the 'round.' A hundred and fifty years* ago, a coterie of Dirdirmen were expelled from the academies at Eliasir and Anismna for the crime of promulgating fantasy. They brought their espousements to Cath, and stimulated a tendentious vogue; the Society of Yearning Refluxives, or the 'cult.' The articles of faith defied established fact. It was asserted that all men, Dirdirmen and sub-men alike, were immigrants from a far planet in the constellation Clari: a paradise where the hopes of humanity have been realized. Enthusiasm for the 'cult' galvanized Cath; a radio transmitter was constructed and signals were projected toward Clari. Somewhere, the activity was resented; someone launched torpedoes which devastated Settra and Ballisidre. The Dirdir are commonly held responsible, but

*The Tschai year: approximately seven-fifths the terrestrial year.

this is absurd; why should they trouble themselves? I assure you that they are much too distant, too uninterested.

"Regardless of agency, the deed was done. Settra and Ballisidre were laid low, the 'cult' was discredited; the Dirdirmen were expelled; the 'round' swung back to orthodoxy. Now even to mention the 'cult' is considered vulgarity, and so we arrive at your case. Clearly you have encountered and assimilated 'cult' dogma; it now manifests itself in your attitudes, your acts, your goals. You seem unable to distinguish fact from fancy. To speak bluntly, you are so disoriented in this regard as to suggest psychic disorder."

Reith closed his mouth on a wild laugh; it would only reinforce Anacho's doubts as to his sanity. A dozen remarks rose to his tongue; he restrained them all. At last he said, "All else aside, I appreciate your candor."

"Not at all," said the Dirdirman serenely. "I imagine that I have clarified the nature of the girl's apprehension."

"Yes," said Reith. "Like yourself she considers me a lunatic."

The Dirdirman blinked up at the pink moon Az. "So long as she was outside the 'round,' at Pera and elsewhere, she made sympathetic allowances. But now return to Cath is imminent . . ." He said no more, and presently went to his couch in the saloon.

Reith went to the forward pulpit under the great bow lantern. A cool draft of air fanned his face; the raft drifted idly about the treetop. From the ground came a furtive crackle of footsteps. Reith listened; they halted, then resumed and diminished off under the trees. Reith looked up into the sky where pink Az, blue Braz careened. He looked back at the deck-house where slept his comrades: a boy of the Emblem nomads, a clown-faced man evolved toward a race of gaunt aliens; a beautiful girl of the Yao, who thought him mad. Below sounded a new pad of footsteps. Perhaps he was mad indeed. . . .

* * *

By morning Reith had recovered his equanimity, and was even able to find grotesque humor in the situation. No good reason to change his plans suggested itself, and the sky-raft limped south as before. The forest dwindled to scrub, and gave way to isolated plantings and cattle-runs, field huts, look-out towers against the approach of nomands, an occasional rutted road. The raft displayed an ever more aggravated instability, with an annoying tendency for the stern to sag. At mid-morning a range of low hills loomed ahead, and the raft refused to climb the few hundred feet necessary to clear the ridge. By the sheerest luck a cleft appeared through which the raft wobbled with ten feet to spare.

Ahead lay the Dwan Zher and Coad: a compact town with a look of settled antiquity. The houses were built of weathered timber, with enormous high-peaked roofs and a multitude of skewed gables, eccentric ridges, dormers, tall chimneys. A dozen ships rode to moorings; as many more were docked across from a row of factors' offices. At the north of town was the caravan terminus, beside a large compound surrounded by hostelries, taverns, warehouses. The compound seemed a convenient spot to set down the raft; Reith doubted if it could have held itself in the air another ten miles.

The raft dropped stern first; the repulsors gave a labored whine and went silent with a meaningful finality. "That's that," said Reith. "I'm glad we've arrived."

The group took up their meager luggage, alighted and left the raft where it had landed.

At the edge of the compound Anacho made inquiries of a dung-merchant and received directions to the Grand Continental, the best of the town's hostelries.

Coad was a busy town. Along the crooked streets, in and out of the ale-colored sunlight, moved men and women of many casts and colors: Yellow Islanders and Black Islanders, Horasin bark-merchants muffled in gray robes; Caucasoids such as Traz from the Aman Steppe; Dirdirmen and Dirdirmen hybrids; dwarfish Sieps from the eastern slopes of the Ojzanalai who played music in the streets; a few flat-faced white men from the far south of Kislovan. The natives, or Tans, were an affable fox-faced people, with wide polished cheek-bones, pointed chins, russet or dark brown hair cut in a ledge across the ears and foreheads. Their usual garments were knee-length breeches, embroidered vest, a round black pie-plate hat. Palanquins were numerous, carried by short gnarled men with oddly long noses and stringy black hair: apparently a race to themselves; Reith saw them in no other occupation. Later he learned them to be natives of Grenie at the head of the Dwan Zher.

On a balcony Reith thought he glimpsed a Dirdir, but he could not be certain. Once Traz grabbed his elbow and pointed to a pair of thin men in loose black trousers, black capes with tall collars all but enveloping their faces, soft cylindrical black hats with wide brims: caricatures of mystery and intrigue. "Pnumekin!" hissed Traz in something between shock and outrage. "Look at them! They walk among other men without a look aside, and their minds full of strange thinking!"

They arrived at the hostelry, a rambling edifice of three stories, with a café on the front veranda, a restaurant in a great tall covered arbor to the rear and balconies overlooking the street. A clerk at a wicket took their money, distributed fanciful keys of black iron as large as their hands and instructed them to their rooms.

"We have traveled a great dusty distance," said Anacho. "We require baths, with good quality unguents, fresh linen, and then we will dine."

"It shall be as you order."

An hour later, clean and refreshed, the four met in the downstairs lobby. Here they were accosted by a black-haired black-eyed man with a pinched melancholy face. He spoke in a gentle voice. "You are newly arrived at Coad?"

Anacho, instantly suspicious, drew himself back. "Not altogether. We are well-known and have no needs."

P. WHALOPIAN '86

"I represent the Slave-taker's Guild, and this is my fair appraisal of your group. The girl is valuable, the boy less so. Dirdirmen are generally considered worthless except in clerical or administrative servitude, for which we have no demand. You would be rated a winkle-gatherer or a nut-huller, of no great value. This man, whatever hs is, appears capable of toil, and would sell for the standard rate. Considering all, your insurance will be ten sequins a week."

"Insurance against what?" demanded Reith.

"Against being taken and sold," murmured the agent. "There is a heavy demand for competent workers. But for ten sequins a week," he declared triumphantly, "you may walk the streets of Coad night and day, secure as though the demon Harasthy rode your shoulders! Should you be sequestered by an unauthorized dealer the Guild will instantly order your free release."

Reith stood back, half-amused, half-disgusted. Anacho spoke in his most nasal voice: "Show me your credentials."

" 'Credentials?' " asked the man, his chin sagging.

"Show us a document, a blazon, a patent. What? You have none? Do you take us for fools? Be off with you!"

The man walked somberly away. Reith asked, "Was he in truth a fraud?"

"One never knows, but the line must be drawn somewhere. Let us eat; I have a good appetite after weeks of steamed pulses and pilgrim plant."

They took seats in the dining room: actually a vast airy arbor with a glass ceiling admitting a pale ivory light. Black vines climbed the walls; in the corners were purple and pale-blue ferns. The day was mild; the end of the room opened to a view of the Dwan Zher and a wind-curled bank of cumulus at the horizon.

The room was half-full; perhaps two dozen people dined from platters and bowls of black wood and red earthenware, talking in low voices, watching the folk at other tables with covert curiosity. Traz looked uneasily here and there, eyebrows raised in disapproval of so much luxury: undoubtedly his first encounter with what must seem a set of faddish and over-complicated niceties, reflected Reith.

He noticed Ylin Ylan staring across the room, as if astonished by what she saw. Almost immediately she averted her eyes, as if uncomfortable and embarrassed. Reith followed her gaze, but saw nothing out of the ordinary. He thought better of inquiring the cause of her perturbation, not wishing to risk a cool stare. And Reith grinned uncomfortably. What a situation: almost as if she were cultivating an active dislike for him! Perfectly comprehensible, of course, if Anacho's explanation were correct. His puzzlement regarding the girl's agitation was now resolved by the sardonic Dirdirman.

"Observe the fellow at the far table," murmured Anacho. "He in the green and purple coat."

Turning his head, Reith saw a handsome young bravo with carefully arranged hair and a rich moustache of a startling gold. He wore elegant garments, somewhat rumpled and well-used: a jacket of soft leather strips, dyed alternately green and purple, breeches of pleated yellow cloth, buckled at knee and ankle with brooches in the shape of fantastic insects. A square cap of soft fur, fringed with two-inch pendants of gold beads slanted across his head; an extravagant garde-nez of gold filigree clung to the ridge of his nose. Anacho muttered, "Watch him now. He will notice us, he will see the girl."

"But who is he?"

Anacho gave his fingertips an irritated twitch. "His name? I do not know. His status: high, in his own opinion at least. He is a Yao cavalier."

Reith turned his attention to Ylin Ylan, who watched the young man from the corner of her eye. Miraculous how her mood had altered! She had become alive and aware, though obviously twitching with nervousness and uncertainty. She flicked a glance toward Reith, and flushed to find his eyes on her. Bending her head she busied herself with the appetizers:

dishes of gray grapes, biscuits, smoked sea-insects, pickled fern-pod. Reith watched the cavalier, who was unenthusiastically dining upon a black seed-bun and dish of pickles, his gaze off across the sea. He gave a sad shrug, as if discouraged by his thoughts, and shifted his position. He saw the Flower of Cath, who feigned the most artless absorption in her food. The cavalier leaned forward in astonishment. He jumped to his feet with such exuberance as nearly to overturn the table. In three long strides he was across the room and down on one knee with a sweeping salute which brushed his cap across Traz's face. "Blue Jade Princess! Your servant Dordolio. My goals are won."

The Flower bowed her head with an exact modicum of restraint and pleased surprise. Reith admired her aplomb. "Pleasant," she murmured, "in a far land to chance upon a cavalier of Cath."

" 'Chance' is not the word! I am one of a dozen who went forth to seek you, to win the boon proclaimed by your father and for the honor of both our palaces. By the wattles of the Pnume's First Devil, it has been given to me to find you!"

Anacho spoke in his blandest voice. "You have searched extensively, then?"

Dordolio stood erect, made a cursory inspection of Anacho, Reith, and Traz, and performed three precise nods. The Flower made a gay little motion, as if the three were casual companions at a picnic. "My loyal henchmen; all have been of incalculable help to me. But for them I doubt if I would be alive."

"In that case," declared the cavalier, "they may ever rely upon the patronage of Dordolio, Gold, and Carnelian. They shall use my field-name Alutrin Stargold." He performed a salute which included all three, then snapped his finger at the serving woman. "A chair, if you please. I will dine at this table."

The serving woman somewhat unceremoniously pushed a chair into place; Dordolio seated himself and gave his attention to the Flower. "But what of your adventures? I assume them to be harrowing. Still you appear as fresh as ever—decidedly unharrowed."

The Flower laughed. "In these steppe-dwellers' garments? I have not yet been able to change. I must buy dozens of sheer necessities before I dare let you look at me."

Dordolio, glancing at her gray garments, made a negligent gesture. "I had noticed nothing. You are as ever. But, if you wish, we will shop together; the bazaars of Coad are fascinating."

"Of course! Tell me of yourself. My father issued a behest, you say?"

"He did indeed, and swore a boon. The most gallant responded. We followed your trail to Spang where we learned who had taken you: Priestesses of the Female Mystery. Many gave you up for lost, but not I. My perseverance has been rewarded! In triumph we will return to Settra!"

Ylin Ylan turned a somewhat cryptic smile toward Reith. "I am of course anxious to return home. What luck to find you here in Coad!"

"Remarkable luck," said Reith dryly. "We arrived only an hour ago from Pera."

"Pera? I do not know the place."

"It lies at the far west of the Dead Steppe."

Dordolio gave an opaque stare, then once more he addressed himself to the Flower. "What hardships you must have suffered! But now you walk under the aegis of Dordolio! We return at once to Settra."

The meal proceeded, Dordolio and Ylin Ylan conversing with great vivacity. Traz, preoccupied with the unfamiliar table implements, turned them dour glances, as if he suspected their ridicule. Anacho paid them no heed; Reith ate in silence. Finally Dordolio sat back in his chair. "Now, as to the practicalities: the packet *Yazilissa* is at mooring, and shortly departs for Vervodei. A melancholy task to take leave of your comrades, good fellows all, I'm sure, but we must arrange our passage home.''

Reith spoke in an even voice. ''All of us, so it happens, are bound for Cath.''

Dordolio presented his blank questioning stare, as if Reith spoke an incomprehensible language.

He rose, helped Ylin Ylan to her feet; the two went to saunter on the terrace beyond the arbor. The serving woman brought the score. ''Five sequins, if you please, for five meals.''

''Five?''

''The Yao ate at your table.''

Reith paid over five sequins from his wallet. Anacho watched in amusement. ''The Yao's presence is actually an advantage; you will avoid attention upon your arrival at Settra.''

''Perhaps,'' said Reith. ''On the other hand, I had hoped for the gratitude of the girl's father. I need all the friends I can find.''

''Events sometimes display a vitality of their own,'' observed Anacho. ''The Dirdir theologists have interesting remarks to make on the subject. I recall an analysis of coincidences—this, incidentally, not by a Dirdir but by a Dirdirman Immaculate . . .'' As Anacho spoke on, Traz went out on the terrace to survey the roofs of Coad; Dordolio and Ylin Ylan walked slowly past, ignoring his presence. Seething with indignation Traz returned to Reith and Anascho. ''The Yao dandy urges her to dismiss us. She refers to us as nomads—rude but honest and dependable.''

''No matter,'' said Reith. ''Her destiny is not ours.''

''But you have practically made it so! We might have remained in Pera, or taken ourselves to the Fortunate Isles; instead—'' He threw up his arms in disgust.

''Events are not occuring as I expected,'' Reith admitted. ''Still, who knows? It may be for the best. Anacho thinks so, at any rate. Would you please ask her to step over here?''

Traz went off on his errand, to return at once. "She and the Yao are off to buy what they call suitable garments? What a farce! I have worn steppe-dwellers' clothes all my life! The garments are suitable and useful."

"Of course," said Reith. "Well, let them do as they wish. Perhaps we also might make a change in our appearance."

Toward the dock area was the bazaar; here Reith, Anacho and Traz fitted themselves out in garments of somewhat less crude cut and material: shirts of soft light linen, short-sleeved vests, loose black breeches buckling at the ankle; shoes of supple gray leather.

The docks were but a few steps away; they continued on to inspect the shipping, and the *Yazilissa* immediately engaged their attention: a three-masted ship over a hundred feet long, with passenger accommodations in a tall many-windowed after-house, and in a row of 'tween-decks cabins along the waist. Cargo booms hung over the docks; bales of goods were hoisted aloft, swung up, over and into the holds.

Climbing the gangplank, they found the supercargo who verified that the *Yazillisa* sailed in three days, touching at ports in Grenie and Horasin, then faring by way of Pag Choda, the Islands of Cloud, Tusa Tula at Cape Gaiz on the western thrust of Kachan, to Vervodei in Cath: a voyage of sixty or seventy days.

Inquiring as to accommodations, Reith learned that all first-class staterooms were booked as far as Tusa Tula, and all but one of the 'tween-decks cabins. There was, however, unlimited deck-class accommodation, which according to the supercargo was not uncomfortable except during the equatorial rains. He admitted these to be frequent.

"Not satisfactory," said Reith. "At the minimum we would want four second-class cabins."

"Unfortunately I can't oblige you unless cancellations come in, which is always possible."

"Very well; I am Adam Reith. You may reach me at the Grand Continental Hotel."

The supercargo stared at him in surprise. " 'Adam Reith?' You and your group are already on the passenger list."

"I'm afraid not," said Reith. "We only arrived in Coad this morning."

"But only an hour ago, perhaps less, a pair of Yao come aboard: a cavalier and a noblewoman. They took accommodations in the name of 'Adam Reith'; the grand suite in the after-house—that is to say, two staterooms with a private saloon—and deck passage for three. I requested a deposit; they stated that Adam Reith would come aboard to pay the passage fee, which is two thousand three hundred sequins. Are you Adam Reith?"

"I am Adam Reith, but I plan to pay no two thousand three hundred sequins. So far as I am concerned, cancel the booking."

"What sort of tomfoolery is this?" demanded the supercargo. "I have no inclination for such frivolity."

"I have even less desire to cross the Draschade Ocean in the rain," said Reith. "If you want recourse, seek out the Yao."

"A pointless exercise," growled the supercargo. "Well then, so be it. If you will be happy with something less than luxury, try aboard the *Vargaz*: the cog yonder. She's departing in a day or so for Cath, and no doubt can find room for you."

"Thank you for your help." Reith and his companions walked down the dock to the *Vargaz*: a short high-pooped round-hulled ship with a long bowsprit, sharply aslant. The two masts supported a pair of lateen yards with sails hanging limp while crewmen sewed on patches of new canvas.

Reith inspected the cog dubiously, then shrugged and went aboard. In the shadow of the after-house two men sat at a table littered with papers, ink-sticks, seals, ribbons and a jug of wine. The most imposing of these was a burly man, naked from the waist up, save for a heavy growth of coarse black hair on his chest. His skin was brown, his features small and hard in a round immobile face. The other man was thin, almost frail, wearing a loose gown of white and a yellow vest the color of his skin. A long moustache drooped sadly beside his mouth; he wore a scimitar at his waist. Ostensibly a pair of sinister ruffians, thought Reith. "Yes, sir, what do you wish?" asked the burly man.

"Transportation to Cath in as much comfort as possible," said Reith.

"Little enough to ask." The man heaved himself to his feet. "I will show you what is available."

Reith eventually paid a deposit on two small cabins for Anacho and Ylin Ylan, a larger stateroom which he would share with Traz. The quarters were neither airy, spacious nor over-clean, but Reith thought that they might have been worse.

"When do you sail?" he asked the burly captain.

"Tomorrow noon on the flood. By preference, be aboard by midmorning; I run a punctual ship."

The three returned through the crooked streets of Coad to the hotel. Neither the Flower nor Dordolio were on the premises. Late in the afternoon they returned in a palanquin, followed by three porters laden with bundles. Dordolio alighted, helped Ylin Ylan forth; they entered the hotel followed by the porters and the chief bearer of the palanquin.

Ylin Ylan wore a graceful gown of dark green silk, with a dark blue bodice. A charming little cap of crystal-frosted net constrained her hair. Seeing Reith she hesitated, turned to Dordolio and spoke a few words. Dordolio pulled at his extraordinary gold moustache, sauntered to where Reith sat with Anacho and Traz.

"All is well," said Dordolio. "I have taken passage for all aboard the *Yazilissa,* a ship of excellent reputation."

"I fear you have incurred an unnecessary expense," said Reith politely. "I have made other arrangements."

Dordolio stood back, nonplussed. "But you should have consulted me!"

"I can't imagine why," said Reith.

"On what ship do you sail?" demanded Dordolio.

"The cog *Vargaz*."

"The *Vargaz*? Bah! A floating pigpen. I would not wish to sail on the *Vargaz*."

"You do not need to do so, if you are sailing on the *Yazilissa*."

Dordolio tugged at his moustache. "The Blue Jade Princess likewise prefers to travel aboard the *Yazilissa*, the best accommodation available."

"You are a bountiful man," said Reith, "to take luxurious passage for so large a group."

"In point of fact, I did only what I could," admitted Dordolio. "Since you are in charge of the group's funds the supercargo will render an account to you."

"By no means," said Reith. "I remind you that I have already taken passage aboard the *Vargaz*."

Dordolio hissed petulantly through his teeth. "This is an insufferable situation."

The porters and the palanquin carrier drew near, and bowed before Reith. "Permit us to tender our accounts."

Reith raised his eyebrows. Was there no limit to Dordolio's insouciance? "Of course, why should you not? Naturally to those who commanded your services." He rose to his feet. He went to Ylin Ylan's room, knocked on the rattan door. There was the sound of movement within; she looked forth through a peep-lens. The upper panel of the door slid back a trifle.

Reith asked, "May I come in?"

"But I'm dressing."

"This has made no difference before."

The door opened; Ylin Ylan stood somewhat sullenly aside. Reith entered. Bundles were everywhere, some opened to reveal garments and leathers, gauze slippers, embroidered bodices, filigree headwear. Reith looked around in astonishment. "Your friend is extravagantly generous."

The Flower started to speak, then bit her lips. "These few things are necessities for the voyage home. I do not care to arrive at Vervodei like a scullery maid." She spoke with a haughtiness Reith had never before heard. "They are to be reckoned as traveling expenses. Please keep an account and father will settle affairs to your satisfaction."

"You put me in a hard position," said Reith, "where inevitably I lose my dignity. If I pay, I'm a lout and a fool; if I don't, I'm a heartless pinchpenny. It seems that you might have handled the situation more tactfully."

"The question of tact did not arise," said the Flower. "I desired the articles. I ordered them to be brought here."

Reith grimaced. "I won't argue the subject. I came to tell you this: I have engaged passage to Cath aboard the cog *Vargaz*, which leaves tomorrow. It is a plain simple ship; you will need plain simple garments."

The Flower stared at him in puzzlement. "But the Noble Gold and Carnelian took passage aboard the *Yazilissa*!"

"If he chooses to travel aboard the *Yazilisa*, he of course may do so, if he can settle for his passage. I have just notified him that I will pay neither for his palanquin rides, nor his passage to Cath, nor"—Reith gestured toward the parcels—"for the finery which he evidently urged you to select."

Ylin Ylan flushed angrily. "I had never expected to find you niggardly."

"The alternative is worse. Dordolio—"

"That is his friend name," said Ylin Ylan in an undertone. "Best that you use his field name, or the formal address: Noble Gold and Carnelian."

"Whatever the situation, the cog *Vargaz* sails tomorrow. You may be aboard or remain in Coad as you choose."

Reith returned to the foyer. The porters and palanquin carrier had departed. Dordolio stood on the front veranda. The jeweled ornaments which had buckled his breeches at the knees were no longer to be seen.

III

THE COG *VARGAZ*, BROAD OF BEAM, WITH HIGH NARROW PROW, a cutaway midships, a lofty stern-castle, wallowed comfortably at its moorings against the dock. Like all else of Tschai, the cog's aspects were exaggerated, with every quality dramatized. The curve of the hull was florid, the bowsprit prodded at the sky, the sails were raffishly patched.

The Flower of Cath silently accompanied Reith, Traz and Anacho the Dirdirman aboard the *Vargaz*, with a porter bringing her luggage on a hand-truck.

Half an hour later Dordolio appeared on the dock. He appraised the *Vargaz* a moment or two, then strolled up the gangplank. He spoke briefly with the captain, tossed a purse upon the table. The captain frowned up sidewise from under bushy black eyebrows, thinking his own thoughts. He opened the purse, counted the sequins and found an insufficiency, which he pointed out. Dordolio wearily reached into his pouch, found the required sum, and the captain jerked his thumb toward the sterncastle.

Dordolio pulled at his moustache, raised his eyes toward the sky. He went to the gangplank, signaled a pair of porters who conveyed aboard his luggage. Then, with a formal bow toward the Flower of Cath, he went to stand at the far rail, looking moodily off across the Dwan Zher.

Five other passengers came aboard: a small fat merchant in a somber gray kaftan and tall cylindrical hat; a man of the Isle of Cloud, with his spouse and two daughters: fresh fragile girls with pale skins and orange hair.

An hour before noon the *Vargaz* hoisted sails, cast off lines, and sheered away from the dock. The roofs of Coad became dark brown prisms laid along the hillside. The crew trimmed sails, coiled down lines, then unshipped a clumsy blast-cannon, which they dragged up to the foredeck.

Reith asked Anacho, "Who do they fear? Pirates?"

"A precaution. So long as a cannon is seen, pirates keep their distance. We have nothing to fear; they are seldom seen on the Draschade. A greater hazard is the victualing. The captain appears a man accustomed to good living, an optimistic sign."

The cog moved easily through the hazy afternoon. The Dwan Zher was calm and showed a pearly luster. The coastline faded away to the north; there were no ships to be seen. Sunset came: a wan display of dove-brown and umber, and with it a cool breeze which sent the water chuckling around the bluff bow.

The evening meal was simple but palatable: slices of dry spiced meat, a salad of raw vegetables, insect paste, pickles, soft white wine from a green glass demijohn. The passengers ate in wary silence; on Tschai strangers were objects of instinctive suspicion. The captain had no such inhibitions. He ate and drank with gusto and regaled the company with witticisms, reminiscences of previous voyages, jocular guesses regarding each passenger's purpose in making the voyage: a performance which gradually thawed the atmosphere. Ylin Ylan ate little. She appraised the two orange-haired girls and became gloomily aware of their appealing fragility. Dordolio sat somewhat apart, paying little heed to the captain's conversation, but from time to time looking sidewise toward the two girls and preening his moustache. After the meal he conducted Ylin Ylan forward to the bow where they watched phosphorescent sea-eels streaking away from the oncoming bow. The others sat on benches along the high quarterdeck, conducting guarded conversations while pink Az and blue Braz rose, one immediately behind the other, to send a pair of trails across the water.

One by one the passengers drifted off to their cabins, and presently the ship was left to the helmsman and the lookout.

Days drifted past; cool mornings with a pearly smoke clinging to the sea; noons with Carina 4269 burning at the zenith; ale-colored afternoons; quiet nights.

The *Vargaz* touched briefly at two small ports along the coast of Horasin: villages submerged in the foliage of giant gray-green trees. The *Vargaz* discharged hides and metal implements, took aboard bales of nuts, lumps of jellied fruit, butts of a beautiful rose and black timber.

Departing Horasin the *Vargaz* veered out into the Draschade Ocean, steering dead east along the equator both to take advantage of the counter-current and to avoid unfavorable weather patterns to the north and south.

Winds were fickle; the *Vargaz* wallowed lazily across almost imperceptible swells.

The passengers amused themselves in their various ways. The orange-haired girls Heizari and Edwe played quoits, and teased Traz until he also joined the game.

Reith introduced the group to shuffleboard, which was taken up with enthusiasm. Palo Barba, the father of the girls, declared himself an instructor of swordsmanship; he and Dordolio fenced an hour or so each day, Dordolio stripped to the waist, a black ribbon confining his hair. Dordolio performed with foot-stamping bravura and staccato exclamations. Palo Barba fenced less flamboyantly, but with great emphasis upon traditional postures. Reith occasionally watched the two at their bouts, and on one occasion accepted Palo

P. W. HAGOPIAN ©'86

Barba's invitation to fence. Reith found the foils somewhat long and over-flexible, but conducted himself without discredit. He noticed Dordolio making critical observations to Ylin Ylan, and later Traz, who had overhead, informed him that Dordolio had pronounced his technique naïve and eccentric.

Reith shrugged and grinned. Dordolio was a man Reith found impossible to take seriously.

Twice other sails were spied in the distance; on one occasion a long black motor-galley changed course in a sinister fashion.

Reith inspected the vessel through his scanscope. A dozen tall, yellow-skinned men wearing complicated black turbans stood looking toward the *Vargaz*. Reith reported as much to the captain, who made a casual gesture. "Pirates. They won't bother us: too much risk."

The galley passed a mile to the south, then turned and disappeared into the southwest.

Two days later an island appeared ahead: a mountainous hump with foreshore cloaked under tall trees. "Gozed," said the captain, in response to Reith's inquiry. "We'll put in for a day or so. You've never touched at Gozed?"

"Never."

"You have a surprise in store. Or then, on the other hand"—here the captain gave Reith a careful inspection—"perhaps you don't. I can't say, since the customs of your own land are unknown to me. And unknown to yourself perhaps? I understand you to be an amnesiac."

Reith made a deprecatory gesture. "I never dispute other people's opinions of myself."

"In itself, a bizarre custom," declared the captain. "Try as I may, I cannot decide the land of your birth. You are a sort strange to me."

"I am a wanderer," said Reith. "A nomad, if you like."

"For a wanderer, you are at times strangely ignorant. Well then, ahead lies Gozed."

The island bulked large against the sky. Looking through

the scanscope Reith could see an area along the foreshore where the trees had been defoliated and trimmed to the condition of crooked poles, each supporting one, two or three round huts. The ground below was barren gray sand, clear of refuse and raked smooth. Anacho the Dirdirman inspected the village through the scanscope. "About what I expected."

"You are acquainted with Gozed? The captain made quite a mystery of the place."

"No mystery. The folk of the island are highly religious; they worship the sea-scorpions native to the waters around the island. They are as large or larger than a man, or so I am told."

"Why then are the huts so high in the air?"

"At night the scorpions come up from the sea to spawn, which they accomplish by stinging eggs into a host animal, often a woman left down on the beach for that purpose. The eggs hatch, the 'Mother of the Gods' is devoured by the larva. In the last stages, when pain and religious ecstasy produce a curious psychological state in the 'Mother,' she runs down the beach and flings herself into the sea."

"An unsettling religion."

The Dirdirman admitted as much. "Still it appears to suit the folk of Gozed. They could change anytime they chose. Sub-men are notoriously susceptible to aberrations of this sort."

Reith could not restrain a grin, and Anancho examined him with surprise. "May I inquire the source of your amusement?"

"It occurs to me that the relationship of Dirdirmen to Dirdir is not unlike that of the Gozed toward their scorpions."

"I fail to see the analogy," Anacho declared rather stiffly.

"Simplicity itself: both are victims to non-human beings who use men for their particular needs."

"Bah!" muttered Anacho. "In many ways you are the most wrong-headed man alive." He walked abruptly aft, to stand staring out over the sea. Pressures were working in Anacho's subconscious, thought Reith, causing him uneasiness.

The *Vargaz* nosed cautiously in toward the beach, swung behind a jut of barnacle-encrusted rock and dropped anchor. The captain went ashore in a pinnace; the passengers saw him talking to a group of stern-faced men, white-skinned, totally naked save for sandals and fillets holding down their long iron-colored hair.

Agreement was reached; the captain returned to the *Vargaz*. A half hour later a pair of lighters came out to the boat. A boom was rigged; bales of fiber and coils of rope were brought aboard; other bales and crates were lowered to the lighters. Two hours after arriving at Gozed the *Vargaz* backed sail, hoisted anchor and set off across the Draschade.

After the evening meal the passengers sat on the deck forward of the sterncastle with a lantern swinging overhead, and the talk veered to the people of Gozed and their religion. Val Dal Barba, wife of Palo Barba, mother of Heizari and Edwe, thought the ritual unjust.

"Why are there only 'Mothers of Gods'? Why shouldn't those flint-faced men go down on the beach and become 'Fathers of Gods'?"

The captain chuckled. "It seems as if the honors are reserved for the ladies."

"It would never be thus in Murgen," declared the merchant warmly. "We pay sizable tithes to the priests; they take all responsibility for appeasing Bisme; we have no further inconvenience."

"A system as sensible as any," agreed Palo Barba. "This year we subscribe to the Pansogmatic Gnosis, and the religion has much virtue to it."

"I like it much better than Tutelanics," said Edwe. "You merely recite the litany and then you are done for the day."

"Tutelanics was a dreadful bore," Heizari concurred. "All that memorizing! And remember that dreadful Convocation of Souls, where the priests were so familiar? I like Pansogmatic Gnosis much better."

Dordolio gave an indulgent laugh. "You prefer not to

become intense. I myself incline in this direction. Yao doctrine, of course, is to some extent a syncresis; or, better to say, in the course of the 'round' all aspects of the Ineffable are given opportunity to manifest themselves, so that, as we move with the cycle, we experience all theopathy."

Anacho, still smarting from Reith's comparisons, looked across the deck. "Well then, what of Adam Reith, the erudite ethnologist? What theosophical insights can he contribute?"

"None," said Reith. "Very few, at any rate. It occurs to me that the man and his religion are one and the same thing. The unknown exists. Each man projects on the blankness the shape of his own particular world-view. He endows his creation with his personal volitions and attitudes. The religious man stating his case is in essence explaining himself. When a fanatic is contradicted he feels a threat to his own existence: he reacts violently."

"Interesting!" declared the fat merchant. "And the atheist?"

"He projects no image upon the blank whatever. The cosmic mysteries he accepts as things in themselves; he feels no need to hang a more or less human mask upon them. Otherwise, the correlation between a man and the shape into which he molds the unknown for greater ease of manipulation is exact."

The captain raised his goblet of wine against the light of the lantern, tossed it down his throat. "Perhaps you're right, but no one will ever change himself on this account. I have known a multitude of peoples. I have walked under Dirdir spires, through Blue Chasch gardens and Wankh castles. I know these folk and their changeling men. I have traveled to six continents of Tschai; I have befriended a thousand men, caressed a thousand women, killed a thousand enemies; I know the Yao, the Binth, the Walalukians, the Schemolei on one hand; on the other the steppe nomads, the marshmen, the islanders, the cannibals of Rakh and Kislovan; I see differences; I see identities. All try to extract a maximum advantage from existence, and finally all die. None seems the better for it. My own God? Good old *Vargaz*! Of course! As Adam Reith insists, it is myself. When *Vargaz* groans through the storm waves, I shudder and grind my teeth. When we glide the dark water under the pink and blue moons, I play the lute, I wear a red ribbon around my forehead, I drink wine. I and *Vargaz* serve each other and the day *Vargaz* sinks into the deep, I sink with her."

"Bravo!" cried Palo Barba, the swordsman, who had also drank much wine. "Do you know, this is my creed as well?" He snatched up a sword, held it high so that lantern-light played up and down its spine. "What the *Vargaz* is to the captain, the sword is to me!"

"Father!" cried his orange-haired daughter Edwe. "And all the time we thought you a sensible Pansogmatist!"

"Please put down the steel," urged Val Dal Barba, "before you become excited and cut someone's ear off."

"What? Me? A veteran swordsman? How can you imagine such a thing? Well then, as you wish. I'll trade the steel for another goblet of wine."

The talk proceeded. Dordolio swaggered across the deck to stand near Reith. Presently he said, in a voice of facetious condescension, "A surprise to find a nomad so accomplished in disquisition, so apt in subtle distinctions."

Reith grinned at Traz. "Nomads are not necessarily buffoons."

"You perplex me," Dordolio declared. "Exactly which is your native steppe? What was your tribe?"

"My steppe is far away; my tribe is scattered in every direction."

Dordolio pulled thoughtfully at his moustache. "The Dirdirman believes you to be an amnesiac. According to the Blue Jade Princess you have implied yourself to be a man from another world. The nomad boy, who knows you best, says nothing. I admit to what may be an obtrusive curiosity."

"The quality signifies an active mind," said Reith.

"Yes, yes. Let me put what I freely acknowledge to be an

absurd question.'' Dordolio examined Reith cautiously sidewise. ''Do you consider yourself to be the native of another world?''

Reith laughed and groped for an answer. He said: ''Four possible conditions exist. If I were indeed from another world I could answer either yes or no. If I were not from another world I could answer yes or no. The first case leads to inconvenience. The second diminishes my self-respect. The third is insanity. The fourth represents the only situation you would not consider an abnormality. The question, hence, as you admit, is absurd.''

Dordolio tugged angrily at his moustache. ''Are you, by any farfetched chance, a member of the 'cult'?''

''Probably not. Which 'cult' is this?''

''The Yearning Refluxives who rode up the cycle to destroy our two gorgeous cities.''

''But I understood that an unknown agency torpedoed the cities.''

''No matter; the 'cult' instigated the attack; they are the cause.''

Reith shook his head. ''Incomprehensible! An enemy destroys your cities; your bitterness is directed not against the cruel enemy but against a possibly sincere and thoughtful group of your own people. A displaced emotion, or so it seems.''

Dordolio gave Reith a cold inspection. ''Your analyses at times border upon the mordant.''

Reith laughed. ''Let it pass. I know nothing of your 'cult.' As for my place of origin, I prefer to be amnesiac.''

''A curious lapse, when otherwise you seem so emphatic in your opinions.''

''I wonder why you trouble tp press the point,'' Reith mused. ''For instance, what would you say if I claimed origin from a far world?''

Dordolio pursed his lips, blinked up at the lantern. ''I had not taken my thoughts quite so far. Well, we will not pursue the subject. A frightening idea, to begin with: an ancient world of men!"

" 'Frightening?' How so?"

Dordolio gave an uneasy laugh. "There is a dark side to humanity, which is like a stone pressed into the mold. The upper side, exposed to sun and air, is clean; tilt it and look below, at the muck and scurrying insects. . . . We of Yao know this well; nothing will put an end to *awaile*. But enough of such talk!" Dordolio gave his shoulders a jerk and a shake, and resumed his somewhat condescending tone of voice. "You are resolved to come to Cath; what will you do there?"

"I don't know. I must exist somewhere; why not in Cath?"

"Not too simple for a stranger," said Dordolio. "Affiliation with a palace is difficult."

"Odd that you should say that! The Flower of Cath declares that her father will welcome us to Blue Jade Palace."

"He would necessarily show formal courtesy, but you could no more take up residence at the Blue Jade Palace than you could on the bottom of the Draschade, merely because a fish invited you to swim."

"What would prevent me?"

Dordolio shrugged. "No man cares to make a fool of himself. Deportment is the definition of life. What does a nomad know of deportment?"

Reith had nothing to say to this. "A thousand details go into the conduct of a cavalier," stated Dordolio, "At the academy we learn degrees of address, signals, language configuration, in which I admit a deficiency. We take instruction in sword address and principles of dueling, genealogy, heraldry; we learn the niceties of costume and a hundred other details. Perhaps you consider these matters over-arbitrary?"

Anacho the Dirdirman, standing nearby, chose to reply. " 'Trivial' is a word more apt."

Reith expected an icy retort, at the least a glare, but Dordolio gave only an indifferent shrug. "Well, then, is your life more significant? Or that of the merchant, or the swordsman? Never forget the Yao are a pessimistic race! *Awaile* is always a threat; we are perhaps more somber than we seem. Recognizing the essential pointlessness of existence, we exalt the small flicker of vitality at our command; we extract the fullest and most distinctive flavor from every incident, by insisting upon an appropriate formality. Triviality? Decadence? Who can do better?''

''All very well,'' said Reith. ''But why be satisfied with pessimism? Why not expand your horizons? Further, it seems that you accept the destruction of your cities with a surprising nonchalance. Vengeance is not the most noble activity, but submissiveness is worse.''

''Bah,'' muttered Dordolio. ''How could a barbarian understand the disaster and its aftermath? The Refluxives in vast numbers took refuge in *awaile*; the acts and the expiations kept our land in a ferment. There was no energy for anything else. Were you of good caste, I would cut your heart out for daring so gross an imputation.''

Reith laughed. ''Since my low caste protects me from retribution, let me ask another question: What is *awaile*?''

Dordolio threw his hands in the air. ''An amnesiac as well as a barbarian! I have no conversation for such as you! Ask the Dirdirman: he is glib enough.'' And Dordolio strode off in a rage.

''An unreasonable display of emotion,'' mused Reith. ''I wonder what my imputation was?''

''Shame,'' said Anacho. ''The Yao are as sensitive to shame as an eyeball to grit. Mysterious enemies destroy their cities; they suspect the Dirdir but dare no recourse, and must cope with helpless rage and shame. It is their typical attribute and predisposes them to *awaile*.''

''And this is?''

''Murder. The afflicted person—one who feels shame—kills as many persons as he is able, of any sex, age or degree of relationship. Then, when he is able to kill no more, he submits and becomes apathetic. His punishment is dreadful and highly dramatic, and enlightens the entire population, who crowd the place of punishment. Each execution has its particular flavor and style and is essentially a dramatic pageant of pain, possibly enjoyed even by the victim. The institution permeates the life of Cath. The Dirdir on this basis consider all sub-men mad."

Reith grunted. "So then, if we visit Cath, we risk insensate murder."

"Small risk. After all, the acts are not ordinary events." Anacho looked around the deck. "But it seems that the hour is late." He bade Reith goodnight and stalked off to his bunk.

Reith remained by the rail, looking out over the water. After the bloodletting at Pera, Cath had seemed a haven, a civilized environment where just possibly he might contrive to patch together a spaceboat. The prospect seemed ever more remote.

Someone came to stand beside him: Heizari, the older of Palo Barba's orange-haired daughters. "You seem so melancholy. What troubles you?"

Reith looked down into the pale oval of the girl's face: an arch impudent face, at this moment alive with innocent—or not so innocent?—coquetry. Reith restrained the first words that rose to his lips. The girl was unquestionably appealing. "How is it you are not in bed with your sister Edwe?"

"Oh, simple! She is not in bed either. She sits with your friend Traz on the quarterdeck, beguiling and provoking, teasing and tormenting. She is much more of a flirt than I."

Poor Traz, thought Reith. He asked, "What of your father and mother? Are they not concerned?"

"What's it to them? When they were young, they dallied as ardently as any; is that not their right?"

"I suppose so. Customs vary, as you know."

"What of you? What are the customs of your people?"

''Ambiguous and rather complicated,'' said Reith. ''There's a great deal of variation.''

''This is the case with Cloud Islanders,'' said Heizari, leaning somewhat closer. ''We are by no means automatically amorous. But on occasion a certain mood comes over a person, which I believe to be the consequence of natural law.''

''No argument there.'' Reith obeyed his impulse and kissed the piquant face. ''Still, I don't care to antagonize your father, natural law or not. He is an expert swordsman.''

''Have no fears on that score. If you require assurance, doubtless he is still awake.''

''I don't know quite what I'd ask him,'' said Reith, ''Well then, all things considered . . .'' The two strolled forward and climbed the carved steps to the forepeak, and stood looking south across the sea. Az hung low in the west laying a line of amethyst prisms along the water. An orange-haired girl, a purple moon, a fairy-tale cog on a remote ocean: would he trade it all to be back on Earth? The answer had to be yes. And yet, why deny the attractions of the moment? Reith kissed the girl somewhat more fervently than before and now from the shadow of the anchor windless, a person hitherto invisible jumped erect and departed in desperate haste. In the slanting moonlight Reith recognized Ylin Ylan, the Flower of Cath. . . . His ardor was quenched; he looked miserably aft. And yet, why feel guilt? She had long since made it clear that the one-time relationship was at an end. Reith turned back to the orange-haired Heizari.

IV

THE MORNING DAWNED WITHOUT WIND. THE SUN ROSE INTO A bird's-egg sky: beige and dove-gray around the horizon, pale gray-blue at the zenith.

The morning meal, as usual, was coarse bread, salt fish, preserved fruit, and acrid tea. The company sat in silence, each occupied with morning thoughts.

The Flower of Cath was late. She slipped quietly into the saloon and took her place with a polite smile to left and right, and ate in a kind of reverie. Dordolio watched her with perplexity.

The captain looked in from the deck. "A day of calm. Tonight clouds and thunder. Tomorrow? No way of knowing. Unusual weather!"

Reith irritably forced himself to his usual conduct. No cause for misgivings: he had not changed; Ylin Ylan had changed. Even at the most intense stage of their relationship she had at all times kept part of herself secret: a persona represented by another of her many names? Reith forced her from his mind.

Ylin Ylan wasted no time in the saloon, but went out on deck, where she was joined by Dordolio. They leaned on the rail, Ylin Ylan speaking with great urgency, Dordolio pulling his moustache and occasionally interposing a word or two.

A seaman on the quarterdeck gave a sudden call and pointed across the water. Jumping up on the hatch Reith saw a dark floating shape, with a head and narrow shoulders, disturbingly manlike; the creature surged, disappeared below the surface. Reith turned to Anacho. "What was that?"

"A Pnume."

"So far from land?"

"Why not? They are the same sort as the Phung. Who holds a Phung to account for his deeds?"

"But what does it do out here, in mid-ocean?"

"Perhaps it floats by night on the surface, watching the moons swing by."

The morning passed. Traz and the two girls played quoits. The merchant mused through a leather-bound book. Palo Barba and Dordolio fenced for a period, Dordolio as usual flamboyant, whistling his steel through the air, stamping his feet, flourishing his arms.

Palo Barba presently tired of the sport. Dordolio stood twitching his blade. Ylin Ylan came to sit on the hatch. Dordolio turned to Reith. "Come, nomad, take up a foil; show me the skills of your native steppe."

Reith instantly became wary. "They are very few; additionally I am out of practice. Perhaps another day."

"Come, come," cried Dordolio, eyes glittering. "I have heard reports of your adroitness. You must not refuse to demonstrate your technique."

"You must excuse me; I am disinclined."

"Yes, Adam Reith!" called Ylin Ylan. "Fence! You will disappoint us all!"

Reith turned his head, examined the Flower for a long moment. Her face, pinched and wan and quivering with emotion, was not the face of the girl he had known in Pera. In some fashion, change had come; he looked into the face of a stranger.

Reith turned his attention back to Dordolio, who evidently had been incited by the Flower of Cath. Whatever they planned was not to his advantage.

Palo Barba intervened, "Come," he told Dordolio. "Let the man rest. I will play another set of passes, and give you all the exercise you require."

"But I wish to engage this fellow," declared Dordolio. "His attitudes are exasperating; I feel that he needs to be chastened."

"If you intend to pick a quarrel," said Palo Barba coldly, "that of course is your own affair."

"No quarrel," declared Dordolio in a brassy, somewhat nasal voice. "A demonstration, let us say. The fellow seems to equate the caste of Cath with common ruck. A significant difference exists, as I wish to make clear."

Reith wearily rose to his feet. "Very well. What do you have in mind for your demonstration?"

"Foils, swords, as you wish. Since you are ignorant of chivalrous address, there shall be none; a simple 'go' must suffice."

"And 'stop'?"

Dordolio grinned through his moustache. "As circumstances dictate."

"Very well." He turned to Palo Barba. "Allow me to look over your weapons, if you please."

Palo Barba opened his box. Reith selected a pair of short light blades.

Dordolio stared, eyebrows arched high in distaste. "Child's weapons, for the training of boys!"

Reith hefted one of the blades, twitched it through the air. "This suits me well enough. If you are dissatisfied, use whatever blade you like."

Dordolio grudgingly took up the light blade. "It has no life; it is without movement or backsnap—"

Reith lifted his sword, tilted Dordolio's hat down over his eyes. "But responsive and serviceable, as you see."

Dordolio removed the hat without comment, shot the cuffs of his white silk blouse. "Are you ready?"

"Whenever you are."

Dordolio raised his sword in a preposterous salute, bowed right and left to the spectators. Reith drew back. "I thought you planned to forgo the ceremonies."

Dordolio merely drew back the corners of his mouth, to show his teeth, and performed one of his foot-stamping assaults. Reith parried without difficulty, feinted Dordolio out of position and swung down at one of the clasps which supported Dordolio's breeches.

Dordolio jumped back, then attacked once more, the snarl replaced by a sinister grin. He stormed Reith's defense, picking here and there, testing, probing; Reith reacted sluggishly. Dordolio feinted, drew Reith's blade aside, lunged. Reith had already jumped away; Dordolio's blade met empty air. Reith hacked down hard at the clasp, breaking it loose.

Dordolio drew back with a frown. Reith stepped forward, struck down at the other clasp, and Dordolio's breeches grew loose about the waist.

Dordolio retreated, red in the face. He cast down the sword. "These ridiculous playthings! Take up a real sword!"

"Use any sword you prefer. I will remain with this one. But, first, I suggest that you take steps to support your trousers; you will embarrass both of us."

Dordolio bowed, with icy good grace. He went somewhat apart, tied his breeches to his belt with thongs. "I am ready. Since you insist, and since my purposes are punitive, I will use the weapon with which I am familiar."

"As you like."

Dordolio took up his long supple blade, flourished it around his head so that it sang in the air, then, nodding to Reith, came to the attack. The flexible tip swung in from right and left; Reith slid it away, and casually, almost as if by accident, tapped Dordolio's cheek with the flat of his blade.

Dordolio blinked, and launched a furious prancing attack.

Reith gave ground; Dordolio followed, stamping, lunging, cutting, striking from all sides. Reith parried, and tapped Dordolio's other cheek. He then drew back. "I find myself winded; perhaps you have had enough exercise for the day?"

Dordolio stood glaring, nostrils distended, chest rising and falling. He turned away, gazed out to sea. He heaved a deep sigh, and turned back. "Yes," he said in a dull voice. "We have exercised enough." He looked down at his jeweled rapier, and for a moment appeared ready to cast it into the sea. Instead, he thrust it into his sheath, bowed to Reith. "Your swordplay is excellent. I am indebted for the demonstration."

Palo Barba came forward. "Well spoken; a true cavalier of Cath! Enough of blades and metal; let us take a goblet of morning wine."

Dordolio bowed. "Presently." He went off to his cabin. The Flower of Cath sat as if carved from stone.

Heizari brought Reith a goblet of wine. "I have a wonderful idea."

"Which is?"

"You must leave the ship at Wyness, come to Orchard Hill and assist at my father's fencing academy. An easy life, without worries or fear."

"The prospect is pleasant," said Reith. "I wish I could . . . but I have other responsibilities."

"Put them aside! Are responsibilities so important when one has a single life to live? But don't answer." She put her hand on Reith's mouth. "I know what you will say. You are a strange man, Adam Reith, so grim and so easy all at once."

"I don't seem strange to myself. Tschai is strange; I'm quite ordinary."

"Of course not!" laughed Heizari. "Tschai is—" She made a vague gesture. "Sometimes it is terrible . . . but strange? I know no other place." She rose to her feet. "Well then, I will pour you more wine and perhaps I will drink as well. On so quiet a day what else is there to do?''

The captain passing near, halted. ''Enjoy the calm while you can; winds are coming. Look to the north.''

On the horizon hung a bank of black clouds; the sea below glimmered like copper. Even as they watched a breath of air came across the sea, a curiously cool waft. The sails of the *Vargaz* flapped; the rigging creaked.

From the cabin came Dordolio. He had changed his garments; now he wore a suit of somber maroon, black velvet shoes, a billed hat of black velvet. He looked for Ylin Ylan; where was she? Far forward on the forepeak, she leaned on the rail, looking off to sea. Dordolio hesitated, then slowly turned away. Palo Barba handed him a goblet of wine; Dordolio silently took a seat under the great brass lantern.

The bank of clouds rolled south, giving off flashes of purple light, and presently the low grumble of thunder reached the *Vargaz*.

The lateen sails were furled; the cog moved sluggishly on a small square storm sail.

Sunset was an eerie scene, the dark brown sun shining under black clouds. The Flower of Cath came from the sterncastle: stark naked she stood, looking up and down the decks, into the amazed faces of the passengers.

She held a dart pistol in one hand, a dagger in the other. Her face was set in a peculiar fixed smile; Reith, who had known the face under a host of circumstances, would never have recognized it. Dordolio, giving an inarticulate bellow, ran forward.

The Flower of Cath aimed the pistol at him; Dordolio dodged; the dart sang past his head. She searched the deck; she spied Heizari, and stepped forward, pistol at the ready. Heizari cried out in fear, ran behind the mainmast. Lightning sprang from cloud to cloud; in the purple glare Dordolio sprang upon the Flower; she slashed him with the dagger; Dordolio staggered back with blood squirting from his neck.

The Flower aimed the dart-gun, Drodolio rolled over behind the hatch. Heizari ran forward to the forecastle; the Flower pursued. A crewman emerged from the forecastle—to stand petrified. The Flower stabbed up into his astounded face; the man tumbled backward, down the companion-way.

Heizari stood behind the foremast. Lightning spattered across the sky; thunder came almost at once.

The Flower stabbed deftly around the mast; the orange-haired girl clutched her side, tottered forth with a wondering face. The Flower aimed the dart gun but Palo Barba was there to knock it clattering to the deck. The Flower cut at him, cut at Reith who was trying to seize her, ran up the ladder to the forepeak, climbed out on the sprit.

The cog rose to the waves; the sprit reared and plunged. The sun sank into the ocean; the Flower turned to watch it, hanging to the forestay with one arm.

Reith called to her, "Come back, come back!"

She turned, looked at him, her face remote. "Derl!" called Reith. "Ylin Ylan!" The girl gave no signal she had heard. Reith called her other names: "Blue Jade Flower!" Then her court name: "Shar Zarin!"

She only gave him a regretful smile.

Reith sought to coax her. He used her child name: "Zozi . . . Zozi . . . come back here."

The girl's face changed. She pulled herself closer to the stay, hugging it.

"Zozi! Won't you talk to me? Come here, there's a good girl."

But her mind was far away, off where the sun was setting.

Reith called her secret name: "L'lae! Come, come here! Ktan calls you, L'lae!"

Again she shook her head, never taking her eyes from the sea.

Reith called the final name though it felt strange to his lips: her love name. He called, but thunder drowned the sound of his voice, and the girl did not hear. The sun was a small

P.W. HAGOPIAN ©86

segment, swimming with antique colors. The Flower stepped from the sprit, and dropped into a hissing surge of spume. For an instant Reith thought he saw the spiral of her dark hair, and then she was gone.

Later, in the evening, with the *Vargaz* pitching up the great slopes and wallowing in a rush down into the troughs, Reith put a question to Ankhe at afram Anacho, the Dirdirman. "Had she simply lost her reason? Or was that *awaile*?"

"It was *awaile*. The refuge from shame."

"But—" Reith started to speak, but could only make an inarticulate gesture.

"You gave attendance to the Cloud Isle girl. Her champion made a fool of himself. Humiliation lay across the future. She would have killed us all had she been able."

"I find it incomprehensible," muttered Reith.

"Naturally. You are not Yao. For the Blue Jade Princess, the pressure was too great. She is lucky. In Settra she would have been punished at a dramatic public torturing."

Reith groped his way out on deck. The brass lantern creaked as if swung. Reith looked out over the blowing sea. Somewhere far away and deep, a white body floated in the dark.

V

FREAKISH WINDS BLEW THROUGHOUT THE NIGHT: GUSTS, BREATHS, blasts, whispers. Dawn brought an abrupt calm, and the sun found the *Vargaz* wallowing in a confused sea.

At noon a terrible squall sent the ship scudding south like a toy, the bluff bow battering the sea to froth. The passengers kept to the saloon, or to the trunk deck. Heizari, bandaged and pale, kept to the cabin she shared with Edwe. Reith sat with her for an hour. She could speak of nothing but her terrible experience. "But why should she do so dreadful a deed?"

"Apparently the Yao are prone to such acts."

"I have heard as much; but even insanity has a reason."

"The Dirdirman says she was overwhelmed by shame."

"What folly! A person as beautiful as she? What could she have done to affect her so?"

"I wouldn't care to speculate," muttered Reith.

The squalls became gigantic hills lofting the *Vargaz* high, heaving the round hull bubbling and singing down the long slopes. Finally one morning the sun shone down from a dove-brown sky clean of clouds. The seas persisted a day longer, then gradually lessened, and the cog set all sail before a fair breeze from the west.

Three days later a dim black island loomed in the south, which the captain declared to be the haunt of corsairs; he kept a sharp lookout from the masthead until the island had merged into the murk of evening.

The days passed without distinguishing characteristic: curiously antiseptic days overshadowed by the uncertainty of the future. Reith became edgy and nervous. How long ago had been the events at Pera: a time so innocent and uncomplicated! At that time, Cath had seemed a haven of civilized security, with Reith certain that the Blue Jade Lord through gratitude would facilitate his plans. What a callow hope!

The cog approached the coast of Kachan, where the captain hoped to ride north-flowing currents up into the Parapan.

One morning, coming on deck, Reith found a remarkable island standing off the starboard beam: a place of no great extent, less than a quarter-mile in diameter, surrounded at the water's edge by a wall of black glass a hundred feet high. Beyond rose a dozen massive buildings of various heights and graceless proportion.

Anacho the Dirdirman came to stand beside him, narrow shoulders hunched, long face dour. "There you see the stronghold of an evil race: the Wankh."

" 'Evil'? Because they are at war with the Dirdir?"

"Because they will not end the war. What benefit to either Dirdir or Wankh is such a confrontation? The Dirdir offer disengagement; the Wankh refuse. A harsh inscrutable people!"

"Naturally, I know nothing of the issues," said Reith. "Why the wall around the island?"

"To daunt the Pnume, who infest Tschai like rats. The Wankh are not a companionable folk. In fact—look down yonder below the surface."

Reith, peering into the water, saw gliding beside the ship at the depth of ten or fifteen feet a dark man-like shape, with a metal structure fixed across its mid-body, moving without motion of its own. The figure twisted, slanted away and vanished into the murk.

P.W. HALOPIAN©86

"An amphibious race, the Wankh, with electric jets for their underwater sport."

Reith once more raised the scanscope. The Wankh towers, like the walls, were black glass. Round windows were disks blacker than black; balconies of frail twisted crystal became walkways to far structures. Reith spied movement: a pair of Wankh? Looking more closely he saw the creatures to be men—Wankhmen, beyond all doubt—with flour-white skins and black pelts close to somewhat flat scalps. Their faces seemed smooth, with still, saturnine features; they wore what appeared to be one-piece black garments, with wide black leather belts, on which hung small implements, tools, instruments. As they moved into the building, they looked out at the *Vargaz* and for an instant Reith saw full into their faces. He jerked the scanscope from his eyes.

Anacho eyed him askance. "What is the trouble?"

"I saw two Wankhmen. . . . Even you, weird mutated freak that you are, seem ordinary by comparison."

Anacho gave a sardonic chuckle. "They are in fact not dissimilar to the typical sub-man."

Reith made no argument; in the first place he could not define the exact quality he had seen behind the still white faces. He looked again, but the Wankhmen had disappeared. Dordolio had come out on deck and now stared in fascination at the scanscope. "What instrument is that?"

"An electronic optical device," said Reith without emphasis.

"I've never seen its like." He looked at Anacho. "Is it a Dirdir machine?"

Anacho made a quizzical dissent. "I think not."

Dordolio gave Reith a puzzled glance. "Is it Chasch or Wankh?" He peered at the engraved escutcheon. "What writing is this?"

Anacho shrugged. "Nothing I can read."

Dordolio asked Reith: "Can you read it?"

"Yes, I believe so." Impelled by a sudden mischievous urge, Reith read:

"Federal Space Agency
Tool and Instrument Division
Mark XI Photomultiplying Binocular Telescope
1X—1000x
Nonprojective, inoperable in total darkness.
BAF-1303-K-29023
Use Type D5 energy slug only. In poor light, engage color compensator switch. Do not look at sun or high-intensity illumination; if automatic light-gate fails, damage to the eyes may result."

Dordolio stared. "What language is that?"

"One of the many human dialects," said Reith.

"But from what region? Men everywhere on Tschai, to my understanding, speak the same language."

"Rather than embarrass you both," said Reith, "I prefer to say nothing. Continue to think of me as an amnesiac."

"Do you take us for fools?" growled Dordolio. "Are we children to have our questions answered with flippant evasions?"

"Sometimes," said Anacho, speaking into the air, "it is the part of wisdom to maintain a myth. Too much knowledge can become a burden."

Dordolio gnawed at his moustache. From the corner of his eye he glanced at the scanscope, then swung abruptly away.

Ahead three more islands had appeared, rising sharply from the sea, each with its wall and core of eccentric black buildings. A shadow lay on the horizon beyond: the mainland of Kachan.

During the afternoon the shadow took on density and detail, to become a hulk of mountains rising from the sea. The *Vargaz* coasted north, almost in the shadow of the mountains, with black dip-winged kites swooping around the masts, emitting mournful hoots and clashing their mandibles. Late in the afternoon the mountains fell away to reveal a land-locked bay. A nondescript town occupied the south shore; from a promontory to the north rose a Wankh fortress, like a growth of undisciplined black crystals. A spaceport occupied the flat land to the east, where a number of spaceships of various styles and sizes were visible.

Through the scanscope, Reith studied the landscape and the mountainside sloping down to the spacefield from the east. *Interesting*, mused Reith, *interesting indeed*.

The captain, coming past, identified the port as Ao Hidis, one of the important Wankh centers. "I had no intent of faring south so far, but since we're here, I'll try to sell my leathers and the Grenie woods; then I'll take on Wankh chemicals for Cath. A word of warning for those of you who intend to roister ashore. There are two towns here: Ao Hidis proper, which is Man-town, and an unpronounceable sound which is Wankh-town. In Man-town are several kinds of people, including Lokhars, but mainly Blacks and Purples. They do not mingle; they recognize their own kind only. In the streets you may walk without fear, you may buy at any shop or booth with an open front. Do not enter any closed shop or tavern, either Black or Purple; you'll likely not come out. There are no public brothels. If you buy from a Black booth, do not stop at a Purple booth with your goods; you will be resented and perhaps insulted, or, in certain cases, attacked. The opposite holds true. As for Wankh-town, there is nothing to do except stare at the Wankh, to which you are welcome, for they do not seem to object. All considered, a dull port, with little amusement ashore."

The *Vargaz* eased alongside a wharf flying a small purple pennon. "I patronized Purple on my last visit," the captain told Reith, who had come up to the quarterdeck. "They gave good service at a fair price; I see no reason to change."

The *Vargaz* was moored by Purple longshoremen: round-faced, round-headed men with a plum-colored cast to their complexion. From the neighboring Black dock Blacks looked on with aloof hostility. These were physiognomically similar to the Purples, but with gray skins oddly mottled with black.

'No one knows the cause,'' remarked the Captain, in regard to the color disparity. ''The same mother may produce one Purple child and one Black. Some blame diet; others drugs; others hold that disease attacks a color-gland in the mother's egg. But Black and Purple they are born; and each calls the other pariah. When Black and Purple breed, the union is sterile, or so it is said. The notion horrifies each race; they would as soon couple with nighthounds.''

''What of the Dirdirman?'' asked Reith. ''Is he likely to be molested?''

''Bah. The Wankh take no notice of such trivia. The Blue Chasch are known for sadistic malice. Dirdir stringencies are unpredictable. But in my experience the Wankh are the most indifferent and remote people of Tschai, and seldom trouble with men. Perhaps they do their evil in secret like Pnume; no one knows. The Wankhmen are a different sort, cold as ghouls, and it is not wise to cross them. Well then, we are docked. Are you going ashore? Remember my warnings; Ao Hidis is a harsh city. Ignore both Black and Purple; talk to no one; interfere with nothing. Last visit I lost a seaman who bought a shawl at a Black shop, then drank wine at a Purple booth. He staggered aboard the ship with foam coming from his nose.''

Anacho chose to remain aboard the *Vargaz*. Reith went ashore with Traz. Crossing the dock they found themselves on a wide street paved with slabs of mica-schist. To either side were houses built crudely of stone and timber, surrounded by rubbish. A few motor vehicles of a type Reith had not previously seen moved along the street; Reith assumed them to be of Wankh manufacture.

Around the shore to the north rose the Wankh towers. In this direction also lay the spaceport.

There seemed to be no public conveyances; Reith and Traz set off on foot. The huts gave way to somewhat more pretentious dwellings, and then they came to a square surrounded on all sides by shops and booths. Half of the folk were

Black, half Purple; nither took notice of the other. Blacks patronized Blacks; Purple shops and booths served Purples. Blacks and Purples jostled each other, without acknowledgement or apology. Detestation hung in the air like a reek.

Reith and Traz crossed the square, continued north along a road paved with concrete, and presently came to a fence of tall grass rods surrounding the spacefield. Reith halted, surveyed the lay of the land.

"I am not naturally a thief," he told Traz. "But notice the little spaceboat! I would gladly confiscate that from its present owner."

"It is a Wankh boat," Traz pointed out pessimistically. "You would not know how to control it."

Reith nodded. "True. But if I had time—a week or so—I could learn. Spacecraft are necessarily similar."

"Think of the practicalities!" Traz admonished him.

Reith concealed a grin. Traz occasionally reverted to the stern personality of Onmale, the near-vital emblem which Traz had worn at the time of their first meeting. Traz shook his head dubiously. "Are valuable vehicles left unattended, ready to fly off into the sky? Unlikely!"

"No one seems to be aboard the small ship," argued Reith. "Even the freighters seem to be empty. Why should there be vigilance? Who would wish to steal them, except a person like myself?"

"Well then, what if you managed to enter the ship?" Traz demanded. "Before you could understand how to operate the machinery, you would be found and killed."

"No question but that the project is risky," agreed Reith.

They returned to the port, and the *Vargaz*, when once more they were aboard, seemed a haven of normalcy.

Cargo was discharged and loaded all during the night. In the morning with all passengers and crew members aboard, the *Vargaz* threw off moorings, hoisted sail and glided back out into the Draschade Ocean.

* * *

The *Vargaz* sailed north under the bleak Kachan coast. On the first day a dozen Wankh keeps appeared ahead, passed abeam and were left in the haze astern. On the second day the *Vargaz* passed in front of three great fjords. From the last of these a motor galley plunged forth, wake churning up astern. The captain immediately sent two men to man the blast-cannon. The galley cut through the swells to pass behind the cog; the captain instantly put about and brought the cannon to bear once more. The galley swung away and off to sea, with the jeers and hoots from the men aboard coming faintly across the water.

A week later Dragan, first of the Isles of Cloud, appeared on the port beam. On the following day the cog put into Wyness; here Palo Barba, his spouse, and his orange-haired daughters disembarked. Traz looked wistfully after them. Edwe turned and waved; then the family was lost to sight among the yellow silks and white linen cloaks of the dockside crowd.

Two days the cog lay at Wyness, unloading cargo, taking on stores and fitting new sails; then the lines were thrown off and the cog put to sea.

With a brisk wind from the west the *Vargaz* drove through the chop of the Parapan. A day passed and a night and another day, and the atmosphere aboard the *Vargaz* became suspenseful, with all hands looking east, trying to locate the loom of Charchan. Evening came; the sun sank into a sad welter of brown and gray and murky orange. The evening meal was a platter of dried fruit and pickled fish, which no one ate, preferring to stand by the rail. The night drew on; the wind lessened; one by one the passengers retired to their cabins. Reith remained on deck, musing upon the circumstances of his life. Time passed. From the quarterdeck came a grummble of orders; the main yard creaked down the mast and the *Vargaz* lost way. Reith went back to the rail. Through the dark glimmered a line of far lights: the coast of Cath.

VI

DAWN REVEALED A LOW-LYING SHORE, BLACK AGAINST THE SEPIA sky. The mainsail was hoisted to the morning breeze; the *Vargaz* moved into the harbor of Vervodei.

The sun rose to reveal the face of the sleeping city. To the north tall flat-faced buildings overlooked the harbor, to the south were wharves and warehouses.

The *Vargaz* dropped anchor; the sails rattled down the mast. A pinnace rowed out with lines and the *Vargaz* was heaved stern-first against a dock. Port officials came aboard, consulted with the captain, exchanged salutes with Dordolio and departed. The voyage was at an end.

Reith bade the captain goodbye, and with Traz and Anacho went ashore. As they stood on the dock Dordolio approached. He spoke in an off-hand voice. "I now take my leave of you, since I depart immediately for Settra."

Wary and wondering as to Dordolio's motives, Reith asked: "The Blue Jade Palace is at Settra?"

"Yes of course." Dordolio pulled at his moustache. "You need not concern yourself in this regard; I will convey all necessary news to the Blue Jade Lord."

"Still, there is much that you do not know," said Reith. "In fact, nearly everything."

"Your information will be of no great consolation," said Dordolio stiffly.

"Perhaps not. But surely he will be interested."

Dordolio shook his head in sad exasperation. "Quixotic! You know nothing of the ceremonies! Do you expect simply to walk up to the Lord and blurt out your tale? Crassness. And your clothes: unsuitable! Not to mention the marmoreal Dirdirman and the nomad lad."

"We must trust to the courtesy and tolerance of the Blue Jade Lord," said Reith.

"Bah," muttered Dordolio. "You have no shame." But still he delayed, frowning off up the street. He said, "You definitely plan to visit Settra then?"

"Yes, of course."

"Accept my advice. Tonight stop at one of the local inns—the Dulvan yonder is adequate—then tomorrow or the next day visit a reputable haberdasher and put yourself into his hands. Then, suitably clothed, come to Settra. The Travelers' Inn on the Oval will furnish you with suitable accommodation. Under these circumstances, perhaps you will do me a service. I seem to have misplaced my funds, and I would be obliged to you for the loan of a hundred sequins to take me to Settra."

"Certainly," said Reith. "But let us all go to Settra together."

Dordolio made a petulant gesture. "I am in haste. Your preparations will consume time."

"Not at all," said Reith. "We are ready at this moment. Lead the way."

Dordolio scanned Reith from head to toe, in vast distaste. "The least I can do, for our mutual comfort, is to see you into respectable clothes. Come along then." He set off along the esplanade toward the center of town. Reith, Traz and Anacho followed, Traz seething with indignation. "Why do we suffer his arrogance?"

"The Yao are a mercurial folk," said Anacho. "Pointless to become disturbed."

Away from the docks the city took on its own character. Wide, somewhat stark streets ran between flat-faced buildings of glazed brick under steep roofs of brown tile. Everywhere a state of genteel dilapidation was evident. The activity of Coad was absent; the few folk abroad carried themselves with self-effacing reserve. Some wore complicated suits, white linen shirts, cravats tied in complex knots and bows. Others, apparently of lesser status, wore loose breeches of green or tan, jackets and blouses of various subdued colors.

Dordolio led the way to a large open-fronted shop, in which several dozen men and women sat sewing garments. Signaling to the three following him, Dordolio entered the shop. Reith, Anacho, and Traz entered and waited while Dordolio spoke energetically to the bald old proprietor.

Dordolio came to confer with Reith. "I have described your needs; the clothier will fit you from his stock, at no large expense."

Three pale young men appeared, wheeling racks of finished garments. The proprietor made swift selection, laid them before Reith, Traz, and Anacho. "These I believe will suit the gentlemen. If they would care to change immediately, the dressing rooms are at hand."

Reith inspected the garments critically. The cloth seemed a trifle coarse; the colors were somewhat raw. Reith glanced at Anacho, whose reflective smile reinforced his own assumptions. Reith said to Dordolio: "Your own clothes are the worse for wear. Why not try on this suit?"

Dordolio stood back with eyebrows raised high. "I am satisfied with what I wear."

Reith put down the garments. "These are not suitable," he told the clothier. "Show me your catalogue, or whatever you work from."

"As you wish, sir."

Reith, with Anacho watching gravely, looked through a

hundred or so color sketches. He pointed to a conservatively cut suit of dark blue. "What of this?"

Dordolio made an impatient sound. "The garments a wealthy vegetable grower might wear to an intimate funeral."

Reith indicated another costume. "What of this?"

"Even less appropriate: the lounge clothes of an elderly philosopher at his country estate."

"Hm. Well then," Reith told the clothier, "show me the clothes a somewhat younger philosopher of impeccable good taste would wear on a casual visit to the city."

Dordolio gave a snort. He started to speak but thought better of it and turned away. The clothier gave orders to his assistants. Reith looked at Anacho with an appraising frown. "For this gentleman, the traveling costume of a high-caste dignitary." And for Traz: "A young gentleman's casual dress."

New garments appeared, conspicuously different from those ordered out by Dordolio. The three changed; the clothier made small adjustments while Dordolio stood to the side, pulling at his moustache. At last he could no longer restrain a comment. "Handsome garments, of course. But are they appropriate? You will puzzle folk when your conduct belies your appearance."

Anacho spoke scornfully: "Would you have us visit Settra dressed like bumpkins? The clothes you selected hardly carried a flattering association."

"What does it matter?" cried Dordolio in a brassy voice. "A fugitive Dirdirman, a nomad boy, a mysterious nonesuch: is it not absurd to trick such folk out in noblemen's costume?"

Reith laughed; Anacho fluttered his fingers; Traz turned Dordolio a glance of infinite disgust. Reith paid the account.

"Now then," muttered Dordolio, "to the airport. Since you demand the best, we shall charter an air-car."

"Not so fast," said Reith. "As usual you miscalculate.

There must be another, less ostentatious means to reach Settra."

"Naturally," said Dordolio with a sneer. "But folk who dress like lords should act like lords."

"We are modest lords," said Reith. He spoke to the clothier. "How do you usually travel to Settra?"

"I am a man with no great regard or 'place';* I ride the public wheelway."

Reith turned back to Dordolio. "If you plan to travel by private air-car, this is where we part."

"Gladly, if you will advance me five hundred sequins."

Reith shook his head. "I think not."

"Then I also must travel by wheelway."

As they strode up the street Dordolio became somewhat more cordial. "You will find that the Yao set great store by consistency, and a harmony of attributes. You are dressed as persons of quality, no doubt you will conduct yourselves in consonance. Affairs will adjust themselves."

At the wheelway depot Dordolio bespoke first-class accommodation from the clerk; a short while later a long car trundled up to the platform, riding a wedge-shaped concrete slot on two great wheels. The four entered a compartment, seated themselves on red plush chairs. With a lurch and a grind, the car left the station and trundled off into the Cath countryside.

Reith found the car intriguing and somewhat of a puzzle. The motors were small, powerful, of sophisticated design; why was the car itself so awkwardly built? The wheels—when the car reached top speed, perhaps seventy miles an hour—rode on cushions of trapped air, at times with silken smoothness, until the wheels came to breaks in the slot, whereupon the car jerked and vibrated abominably. The Yao,

*An untranslatable word: the quality a man acquires in greater or lesser extent by the grace of his evolutions upon aspects of the 'round.' A fragile, almost frivolous, equilibrium between a man and his peers, instantly disturbed by a hint of shame, humiliation, embarrassment.

reflected Reith, seemed to be good theoreticians but poor engineers.

The car rumbled across an ancient cultivated countryside, more civilized than any Reith had yet seen on Tschai. A haze hung in the air, tinting the sunlight antique yellow; shadows were blacker than black. In and out of forests rolled the car, beside orchards of gnarled black-leaved trees, past parks and manors, ruined stone walls, villages in which only half the houses seemed tenanted. After climbing to an upland moor, the car struck east over marshes and bogs, outcrops of rotting limestone. No human being was in sight, though several times Reith thought to discern ruined castles in the distance.

"Ghost country," said Dordolio. "This is Audan Moor; have you heard of it?"

"Never," said Reith.

"A desolate region, as you can see. The haunt of outlaws, even an occasional Phung. After dark the nighthounds bell . . ."

Down from Audan Moor rolled the wheelway car, into a countryside of great charm. Everywhere were ponds and watercourses, overlooked by towering black, brown and rust-colored trees. On small islands stood tall houses with high-pitched gables and elaborate balconies. Dordolio pointed off to the east. "See yonder, the great manse in front of the forest? Gold and Carnelian: the palace of my connections. Behind—but you cannot see—is Halmeur, an outer district of Settra."

The car swung through a forest and came out into a region of scattered farmsteads with the domes and spires of Settra on the sky ahead. A few minutes later the car entered a depot and rolled to a halt. The passengers alighted, and walked to a terrace. Here Dordolio said: "Now I must leave you. Across the Oval you will find the Travelers' Inn, to which I recommend you and where I will send a messenger with the sum of my debt." He paused and cleared his throat. "If a freak of destiny brings us together in another setting—for instance, you have evinced a somewhat unrealistic ambition to make yourself acquainted with the Blue Jade Lord—it might serve our mutual purposes were we not to recognize each other."

"I can think of no reason for wanting to do so," said Reith politely.

Dordolio glanced at him sharply, then made a formal salute. "I wish you good fortune." He walked off across the square, his strides lengthening as he went.

Reith turned to Traz and Anacho. "You two go to the Travelers' Inn, arrange for accommodations. I'm off to the Blue Jade Palace. With any luck I'll arrive before Dordolio, who seems in a peculiar state of haste."

He walked to a line of motorized tricycles, climbed aboard the first in line. "The Blue Jade Palace, with all speed," he told the driver.

The mechanism spun off to the south, past buildings of glazed brick and dim glass panes, then into a district of small timber cottages, then past a great outdoor market, a scene as brisk and variegated as any Reith had observed in Cath. Turning aside, the motor-buggy nosed across an ancient stone bridge, through a portal in a stone wall into a large circular plaza. Around the periphery were booths, for the most part unoccupied and barren of goods; at the center a short ramp led up to a circular platform, at the back of which rose a bank of seats. A rectangular frame occupied the front of the platform, of dimensions which Reith found morbidly suggestive.

"What is this place?" he asked the driver, who gave him a glance of mild wonder.

"The Circle, site of Pathetic Communion, as you can see. You are a stranger in Settra?"

"Yes."

The driver consulted a yellow cardboard schedule. "The next event is Ivensday, when a nineteen-sore comes to clarify his horrible desperation. Nineteen! The most since the twenty-two of Agate Crystal's Lord Wis."

"You mean he killed nineteen?"

"Of course; what else? Four were children, but still a feat

P.W.HAGOPIAN©86

these days when folk are wary of *awaile*. All Settra will come to the expiation. If you're still in town you could hardly do more for your own soul's profit."

"Probably so. How far to Blue Jade Palace?"

"Through Dalmere and we're almost there."

"I'm in a hurry,"said Reith. "As fast as possible."

"Indeed sir, but if I wreck or injure, I'll feel extraordinary shame, to my soul's sickness, and I would not care to risk despondency."

"Understandable."

The motor-buggy spun along a wide boulevard, dodging and veering to avoid potholes. Enormous trees, black-trunked with brown and purple-green foliage, overhung the way; to either side, shrouded in dark gardens, were mansions of the most extraordinary architecture. The driver pointed. "Yonder on the hill: Blue Jade Palace. Which entrance do you favor, sir?" He inspected Reith quizzically.

"Drive to the front," said Reith. "Where else?"

"As you say, your lordship. Although most of the fronters don't arrive in three-wheel motor-buggies."

Up the driveway rolled the vehicle, and under a *porte cochere*, the buggy halted. Paying the fare, Reith alighted upon a silken cloth laid under his feet by a pair of bowing footmen. Reith walked briskly through an open arch into a room paneled with mirrors. Myriad prisms of crystal hung tinkling on silver chains. A majordomo wearing russet velvet livery bowed deeply. "Your lordship is at home. Will you rest or take a cordial, though my Lord Cizante impatiently awaits the privilege of greeting you."

"I will see him at once; I am Adam Reith."

"Lord of which realm?"

"Tell Lord Cizante that I bring important information."

The majordomo looked at Reith uncertainly, his face twisting through a dozen subtle emotions. Reith understood that already he had committed gaucheries. *No matter*, he thought, *the Blue Jade Lord will have to make allowance.*

The majordomo signaled, a trifle less obsequiously than before. "Be good enough to come this way."

Reith was taken into a small court murmuring to a waterfall of luminous green liquid.

Two minutes passed. A young man in green knickers and an elegant waistcoat appeared. His face was wax pale, as if he never saw sunlight; his eyes were somber and brooding; under a loose four-corner cap of soft green velvet his hair was jet black: a man richly handsome, by some extraordinary means contriving to seem both effete and competent. He examined Reith with critical interest, and spoke in a dry voice. "Sir, you claim to have information for the Blue Jade Lord?"

"Yes. Are you he?"

"I am his aide. You may impart your information to me with assurance."

"I have news relating to the fate of his daughter," said Reith. "I prefer to speak to the Blue Jade Lord directly."

The aide made a curious mincing motion and disappeared. Presently he returned. "Your name, sir?"

"Adam Reith."

"Follow me, if you will."

He took Reith into a wainscoted room enameled a brownish ivory, lit by a dozen luminous prisms. At the far end stood a frail frowning man in an extravagant eight-piece suit of black and purple silk. His face was round, dark hair grew down his forehead in an elflock; his eyes were dark, far apart, and his tendency was to glance sidelong. *The face*, thought Reith, *of a secretive suspicious man*. He examined Reith with a compression of the lips.

"Lord Cizante," said the aide, "I bring you the gentleman Adam Reith, heretofore unknown, who, chancing past, was pleased to learn that you were in the vicinity."

There was an expectant silence. Reith understood that the circumstances demanded a ritual response. He said, "I am pleased, naturally, to find Lord Cizante in residence. I have only this hour arrived from Kotan.''

Cizante's mouth tightened, and Reith knew that once again he had made a graceless remark.

Cizante spoke in a crisp voice. ''Indeed. You have news regarding the Lady Shar Zarin?''

This was the Flower's court name. Reith responded in a voice as cool as Cizante's own. ''Yes. I can give you a detailed account of her experiences, and her unfortunate death.''

The Blue Jade Lord looked toward the ceiling and spoke without lowering his eyes. ''You evidently claim the boon?''

The majordomo entered the room, whispered to the aide, who discreetly murmured to Lord Cizante.

''Curious!'' declared Cizante. ''One of the Gold and Carnelian scions, a certain Dordolio, likewise comes to claim the boon.''

''Send him away,'' said Reith. ''His knowledge of the matter is superficial, as you will learn.''

''My daughter is dead?''

''I am sorry to say that she drowned herself, after an attack of psychic malaise.''

The Lord's eyebrows rose more sharply than before. ''She gave way to *awaile*?''

''I would suppose so.''

''When and where did this take place?''

''Three weeks ago, aboard the cog *Vargaz*, halfway across the Draschade.''

Lord Cizante dropped into a chair. Reith waited for an invitation to do likewise, but thought better of seating himself. Lord Cizante spoke in a dry voice: ''Evidently she had suffered deep humiliation.''

''I couldn't say. I helped her escape from the Priestesses of the Female Mystery; thereafter she was secure and under my protection. She was anxious to return to Cath and urged me to accompany her, assuring me of your friendship and gratitude. But as soon as we started westward she became gloomy, and, as I say, halfway across the Draschade she threw herself overboard.''

While Reith spoke Cizante's face had shifted through phases and degrees of various emotions. ''So now,'' he said in a clipped voice, ''with my daughter dead, after circumstances I do not care to imagine, you come hurrying here to claim the boon.''

Reith said coldly, ''I knew then and know nothing now of this 'boon.' I came to Cath for several reasons, the least important of which was to make myself known to you. I find you indisposed to what I consider civilized standards of courtesy and I will now leave.'' Reith gave a curt nod and started for the door. He turned back. ''If you wish to learn further details regarding your daughter, consult Dordolio, whom we found stranded at Coad.''

Reith left the room. The Lord's sibilant murmur reached his ears: ''You are an uncouth fellow.''

In the hall waited the majordomo, who greeted Reith with the faintest of smiles. He indicated a rather dim passageway painted red and blue. ''This way, sir.''

Reith paid him no need. Crossing into the grand foyer, he left the way he had come.

VII

REITH WALKED BACK TOWARD THE OVAL, PONDERING THE CITY Settra and the curious temperament of its people. He was forced to admit that the scheme to build a small spaceboat, which in far-off Pera had appeared at least feasible, now seemed impractical. He had expected gratitude and friendship from the Blue Jade Lord; he had encountered hostility. As to the technical abilties of the Yao, he was inclined to pessimism, and he fell to appraising the vehicles which passed along the street. They appeared to function satisfactorily, though giving the impression that flair and elegance, rather than efficiency, had been first in the minds of the designers. Energy derived from the ubiquitous power cells produced by the Dirdir; the coupling was not altogether quiet: an indication, so Reith considered, of careless or incompetent engineering. No two were alike; each seemed an individual construction.

Almost certainly, reflected Reith, the Yao technology was inadequate to his purposes. Without access to standard components, maxima-minima sets, integrated circuit blocks, structural forms, computers, Fourier analyzers, macro-gauss generators, a thousand other instruments, tools, gauges, standards, not to mention clever and dedicated technical personnel, the construction of even the crudest spaceboat became a stupendous task—impossible in a single lifetime. . . . He came to a small circular park, shadowed under tall psillas with shaggy black bark and leaves of russet paper. At the center rose a massive monument. A dozen male figures, each carrying an instrument or tool, danced in a dreadful ritual grace around a female form, who stood with arms raised high, upturned face twisted in some overpowering emotion. Reith could not identify her expression. Exultation? Agony? Grief? Beatification? Whatever the case, the monument was disturbing, and rasped at a dark corner of his mind like a mouse in the woodwork. The monument seemed very old—thousands of years? Reith could not be sure. A small girl and a somewhat younger boy came last. They paused first to study Reith; then gave fascinated attention to the gliding figures and their macabre instruments. Reith, in a somber mood, continued on his way and presently came to the Travelers' Inn. Neither Traz nor the Dirdirman were on the premises. They had, however, hired accommodations: a suite of four rooms overlooking the Oval.

Reith bathed, changed his linen. When he went down to the foyer, twilight had come to the Oval, which was now lit by a ring of great luminous globes in a variety of pastel colors. Traz and Anacho appeared on the other side of the Oval. Reith watched them with a wry grin. They were basically alien, like cat and dog; yet, when circumstances threw them together, they conducted themselves with cautious good-fellowship.

Anacho and Traz, so it developed, had chanced upon an area known as "the Mall," where cavaliers settled affairs of honor. In the course of the afternoon the two had watched three bouts: near-bloodless affairs, Traz reported with a sniff of scorn. "The ceremonies exhaust their energy," said Anacho. "After the addresses and the punctilio there is little time for fighting."

"The Yao, if anything, are more peculiar than the Dirdirmen," said Reith.

"Ha ha! I dispute that! You know a single Dirdirman. I can show you a thousand and confuse you totally. But come; the refectory is around the corner. If nothing else, the Yao cuisine is satisfactory."

The three dined in a wide room hung with tapestries. As usual Reith could not identify what he ate, and did not care to learn. There was yellow broth, faintly sweet, with floating flakes of pickled bark; slices of pale meat layered with flower petals; a celery-like vegetable crusted with crumbs of a fiery-hot spice; cakes flavored with musk and resin; black berries with a flavor of the swamp; clear white wine which tingled the mouth.

In an adjacent tavern the three took after-dinner liquors. The clientele included many non-Yao folk, who seemed to use the place as a rendezvous. One of these, a tall old man in a leather bonnet, somewhat the worse for drink, peered into Reith's face. "But I'm wrong, for a fact. I thought you a Vect of Holangar; then I asked myself where are his tongs? And I said, no, it is just another of the anomes who creep into Travelers' Inn for a sight of their own kind."

"I'd like a sight of my own kind," said Reith. "Nothing would please me more."

"Yes, isn't this the case? What sort are you, then? I can't put a name to your face."

"A wanderer from far lands."

"No farther than mine, which is the far coast of Vord, where Cape Dread holds back the Schanizade. I have seen sights, I tell you that! Raids on Arkady! Battles with seafolk! I remember an occasion when we drove into the mountains and destroyed the bandits. . . . I was a young man then and a great soldier; now I toil for the ease of the Yao, and earn my own ease thereby, and it is not so hard a life."

"I should suppose not. You are a technician?"

"Nothing so grand. I inspect wheels at the car yard."

"Many foreign technicians are at work in Settra?"

"True. Cath is comfortable enough, if you can overlook the vagaries of the Yao."

"What about Wankhmen? Are there any such in Settra?"

"At work? Never. When I sojourned at Ao Zalil, to the east of Lake Falas, I saw how it went. The Wankhmen will not even work for the Wankh; they have sufficient exertion pronouncing the Wankh chimes. Though usually they play the chords on remarkable little instruments."

"Who works in the Wankh shops? Blacks and Purples?"

"Bah! One might be forced to handle an article the other had touched. Back-country Lokhars for the most part work in the shops. For ten or twenty years, or longer, they toil, then they return to their villages rich men. Wankhmen at work in the shops? What a joke! They are as proud as Dirdirman Immaculates! I see a Dirdirman beside you tonight."

"Yes, he is my comrade."

"Odd to find a Dirdirman so common!" marveled the old man. "I have seen only three previously and all treated me like dirt." He drained his goblet, set it down with a rap. "Now I must leave; I bid all good evening, Dirdirman as well."

The old man departed. With almost the same swing of the door a pale black-haired young man dressed unobtrusively in dark blue broadcloth entered the tavern. Somewhere, thought Reith, he had seen this young man, and recently. . . . Where? The man walked slowly, almost absentmindedly, along the passage beside the wall. He went to the serving counter, was poured a goblet of sharp syrup. As he turned away his gaze met that of Reith's. He nodded politely and after a moment's hesitation approached. Reith now recognized him for Cizante's pallid young aide.

"Good evening," said the young man. "Perhaps you recognize me? I am Helsse of Isan, a Blue Jade connection. I believe that we met today."

"I had a few words with your master, true enough."

Helsse sipped from his goblet, made a fastidious grimace, placed the goblet on the bar. "Let's move to a more seclued place, where we can talk."

Reith spoke to Traz and Anacho, then turned back to Helsse. "Lead the way."

Helsse glanced casually toward the front entrance but chose to leave through the restaurant. As they departed Reith glimpsed a man thrusting into the tavern, to glare wildly around the room: Dordolio.

Helsse appeared not to notice. "Nearby is a little cabaret, not overly genteel, but as good as anywhere else for our talk."

The cabaret was a low-ceilinged room, lit by red and blue lamps with blue painted booths around the periphery. A number of musicians sat on a platform, two of whom played small gongs and drum, while a male dancer strode sinuously this way and that. Helsse selected a booth near the door, as far as possible from the musicians; the two seated themselves on blue cushions. Helsse ordered two drams of "Wildwood Tincture" which were presently brought to the table.

The dancer departed, the musicians undertook a new selection, with instruments similar to oboe, flute, cello, and a kettledrum. Reith listened for a moment, puzzled by the plaintive scraping, the thumps of the kettledrum, the sudden excited trills of the flute.

Helsse leaned solicitously forward. "You are unfamiliar with Yao music? I thought as much. This is one of the traditional forms: a lament."

"It could never be mistaken for a cheerful composition."

"A question of degree." Helsse went on to list a series of musical forms, of decreasing optimism. "I do not mean to imply that the Yao are a dour folk; you need only attend one of the season balls to appreciate this."

"I doubt if I will be invited," said Reith.

The orchestra embarked upon another selection, a series of passionate phrases, taken up by each instrument at varying

P.W. HAGOPIAN©'8

instants, to terminate in a wild sustained quaver. By some cross-sensoral stimulus, Reith thought of the monument in the circular park. "The music bears some connection with your ritual of expiation?"

Helsse smiled distantly. "I have heard it said that the spirit of Pathetic Communion permeates the Yao psyche."

"Interesting." Reith waited. Helsse had not brought him here to discuss music.

"I trust that the events of this afternoon caused you no inconvenience?" asked Helsse.

"None whatever, other than irritation."

"You did not expect the boon?"

"I knew nothing of it. I expected ordinary courtesy, certainly. My reception by Lord Cizante, in retrospect, seems remarkable."

Helsse nodded sagely. "He is a remarkable man. But now he finds himself in an awkward position. Immediately upon your departure the cavalier Dordolio presented himself to denounce you as an interloper, and to demand the boon for himself. To be quite candid, such a proceeding, on Dordolio's terms, would embarrass Lord Cizante, when one takes all into consideration. You perhaps would not be aware that Blue Jade and Gold-Carnelian are rival houses. Lord Cizante suspects that Dordolio would use the boon to humiliate Blue Jade, with what consequences no one can foresee."

Reith asked: "Exactly what was the boon promised by Cizante?"

"Emotion overcame his reserve," said Helsse. "He declared: 'Whoever returns me my daughter or so much as brings me news, let him ask and I will fulfill as best I can.' Strong language, as you see, uttered only for the ears of Blue Jade, but the news circulated."

"It appears," said Reith, "that I do Cizante a favor by accepting his bounty."

"This is what we wish to ascertain," said Helsse carefully. "Dordolio has made a number of scurrilous statements in regard to you. He declares you a superstitious barbarian intent on reviving the 'cult.' If you demanded that Lord Cizante convert his palace into a temple and himself join the 'cult,' he might well prefer Dordolio's terms."

"Even though I appeared first on the scene?"

"Dordolio claims trickery, and is violently angry. But all this to the side, what might you demand of Lord Cizante, in light of the circumstances?"

Reith considered. Unfortunately, he could not afford the prideful luxury of refusal. "I'm not sure. I could use some unprejudiced advice, but I don't know where to find it."

"Try me," suggested Helsse.

"You are hardly unprejudiced."

"Much more than you might think."

Reith studied the pale handsome face, the still black eyes. A puzzling man was Helsse, the more so for his impersonality, neither cordial nor cold. He spoke with ostensible candor but permitted no inadvertent or unconscious signals to advertise the state of his inner self.

The orchestra had dispersed. To the platform came a somewhat obese man in a long maroon robe. Behind him sat a woman with long black hair plucking a lute. The man produced a ululating wail: half-words which Reith was unable to comprehend. "Another traditional melody?" he inquired.

Helsse shrugged. "A special mode of singing. It is not altogether without value. If everyone belabored themselves thusly, there would be far less *awaile*."

Reith listened. "Judge me harshly all," moaned the singer. "I have performed a terrible crime; it is because of my despair."

"Offhand," said Reith, "it seems absurd to discuss my best advantage over Lord Cizante with Cizante's aide."

"Ah, but your best advantage is not necessarily Lord Cizante's disadvantage," said Helsse. "With Dordolio the case is different."

"Lord Cizante showed me no great courtesy," mused

Reith. "I am not anxious to do him a favor. On the other hand, I do not care to assist Dordolio who calls me a superstitious barbarian."

"Lord Cizante was perhaps shocked by your news," suggested Helsse. "As for Dordolio's charge, it is obviously inaccurate and need no longer be considered."

Reith grinned. "Dordolio has known me a month; can you dispute him on the basis of such short acquaintance?"

If he had hoped to discomfit Helsse, he was unsuccessful. Helsse's smile was bland. "I am usually correct in my appraisals."

"Suppose that I were to make a set of apparently wild assertions: that Tschai was flat, that the tenets of the 'cult' were correct, that men could live underwater—what would become of your opinion?"

Helsse considered soberly. "Each case is different. If you told me Tschai was flat, I would certainly revise my judgment. If you argued the creed of the 'cult,' I would suspend a decision and listen to your remarks, for here is a matter of opinion and no evidence exists, at least to my knowledge. If you insisted that men could live underwater I might be inclined to accept the statement as a working premise. After all, the Pnume submerge, as do the Wankh; why not men, perhaps with special equpment?"

"Tschai is not flat," said Reith. "Men are able to live underwater for short periods using artificial gills. I know nothing of the 'cult' or its doctrines."

Helsse sipped from his goblet of essence. The singer had departed; a dance troupe now came forth; men in black leggings and sleeves, nude from upper thigh to rib cage. Reith stared in fascination for a moment or two, then looked away.

"Traditional dances," explained Helsse, "relating to Pathetic Communion. This is 'Precursory Movement of the Ministrants toward the Expiator.' "

"The 'ministrants' are torturers?"

"They are those who provide latitude for absolute expiation. Many become popular heroes because of their passionate techniques." Helsse rose to his feet. "Come. You have implied at least a mild interest in the 'cult.' As it happens, I know the location of their meeting place, which is not far from here. If you are interested, I will take you there."

"If the visit is not contrary to the laws of Cath."

"No fear of that. Cath has no laws, only customs, which seems to suit the Yao well enough."

"Peculiar," said Reith. "Killing is not proscribed?"

"It offends custom, at least under certain circumstances. However, the professional assassins of the Guild and the Service Company work without public reproach. In general the folk of Cath do what they see fit and suffer more or less opprobrium. So you may visit the 'cult' and incur, at the worst, invective."

Reith rose to his feet. "Very well; lead the way."

They walked across the Oval, through a winding alley into a dim avenue. The eccentric silhouettes of the houses opposite leaned across the sky, where Az and Braz both ranged. Helsse rapped at a door displaying a pale blue phosophor. The two men waited in silence. The door opened a crack; a long-nosed face peered forth.

"Visitors," said Helsse. "May we come in?"

"You are associates? I must inform you that here is the distinct center for the Society of Yearning Refluxives."

"We are not associates. This gentleman is an outlander who wishes to learn something of the 'cult.' "

"He is welcome and yourself as well, since you seem to have no concern for 'place.' "

"None whatever."

"Which marks you either the highest of the high or the lowest of the low. Enter then. We have little entertainment to offer—convictions, a few theories, fewer facts." The Refluxive swept aside a curtain. "Enter."

Helsse and Reith stepped into a large low room. To one

side, forlorm in so much vacant space, two men and two women sat drinking tea from iron pots.

The Refluxive made a half-obsequious, half-sardonic gesture. "Here we are; stare yourself full at the dreadful 'cult.' Have you ever seen anything less obstreperous?"

"The 'cult,' " said Helsse, somewhat sententiously, "is despised not for the look of its meeting halls, but for its provocative assumptions."

" 'Assumptions' bah!" declared the Refluxive in a voice of peevish complaint. "The others persecute us but we are the chosen in knowledge."

Reith asked: "What, precisely, do you know?"

"We know that men are strangers to Tschai."

"How can you know this?" demanded Helsse. "Human history fades into murk."

"It is an intuitive Truth. We are equally certain that someday the Human Magi will call their seed back Home! And then what joy! Home is a world of bounty, with air that rejoices in the lungs, like the sweetest Iphthal wine! On Home are golden mountains crowned with opals and forests of dreams! Death is a strange accident, not a fate; all men wander with joy and peace for company, with delicious viands everywhere for the eating!"

"A delightful vision!" said Helsse, "but do you not consider it somewhat conjectural? Or more properly, institutional dogma?"

"Possibly so," declared the stubborn Refluxive. "Still, dogma is not necessarily falsehood. These are revealed truths, and behold: the revealed image of Home!" He pointed to a world globe three feet in diameter hanging at eye-level.

Reith went to inspect the globe, tilting his head this way and that, trying to identify outline of sea and shore, finding here a haunting familiarity, there utter disparity. Helsse came to stand beside him. "What does it look like to you?" His voice was light and careless.

"Nothing in particular."

Helsse gave a soft grunt of mingled relief and perhaps disappointment, or so it seemed to Reith.

One of the women lifted her obese body from the bench and came forward. "Why not join the Society?" she wheedled. "We need new faces, new blood, to augment the vast new tide. Won't you help us make contact with Home?"

Reith laughed. "Is there a practical method?"

"To be sure! Telepathy! Indeed, we have no other recourse."

"Why not a spaceship?"

The woman seemed bewildered, and looked sharply to see if Reith were serious. "Where could we lay our hands on a spaceship?"

"They are nowhere to be bought?" Even a small one?"

"I have never heard of such a case."

"Nor I," was Helsse's dry comment."

"Where would we fare?" demanded the woman, half-truculently. "Home is situated in the constellation Clari, but space is vast; we would drift forever."

"The problems are large," Reith agreed."Still, assuming that your premise is correct—"

" 'Assume?' " 'Premise?' " demanded the fat woman in a shocked voice. 'Revelation,' rather."

"Possibly so. But mysticism is not a practical approach to space travel. Let us suppose that by one means or another, you find yourself in command of a spaceship, then you might very easily verify the basis of your beliefs. Simply fly into the constellation Clari, halting at appropriate intervals to monitor the area for radio signals. Sooner or later, if the world Home exists, a suitable instrument will detect the signals."

"Interesting," said Helsse. "You assume that such a world, if it exists, is sufficiently advanced to propagate these signals?"

Reith shrugged."Since we're assuming the world, why not assume the signals?"

Helsse had nothing to say. The Refluxive declared, "Ingenious but superficial! How, for instance, would we obtain a spaceship?"

"With sufficient funds and technical competence you could build a small vessel."

"To begin with," said the Refluxive, "we have no such funds."

"The least of the difficulties, or so I would think," murmured Helsse.

"The second possibility is to buy a small boat from one of the spacefaring peoples: the Dirdir, the Wankh, or perhaps even the Blue Chasch."

"Again a question of sequins," said the Refluxive. "How much would a spaceboat cost?"

Reith looked at Helsse, who pursed his lips. "Half a million sequins, should anyone be willing to sell, which I doubt."

"The third possibility is the most direct," said Reith. "Confiscation, pure and simple."

"Confiscation? From whom? Though members of the 'cult,' we are not yet lunatics."

The fat woman gave a sniff of disapproval. "The man is a wild romantic."

The Refluxive said gently, "We would gladly accept you as an associate, but you must discover orthodox methodology. Classes in thought-control and projective telepathy are offered twice a week, on Ilsday and Azday. If you care to attend—"

"I'm afraid that this is impossible," said Reith. "But your program is interesting and I hope it brings fruitful returns."

Helsse made a courteous sign; the two departed.

They walked along the quiet avenue in silence. The Helsse inquired: "What is your opinion now?"

"The situation speaks for itself," said Reith.

"You are convinced then that their doctrine is implausible?"

"I would not go quite so far. Scientists have undoubtedly found biological links between Pnume, Phung, nighthounds, and other indigenous creatures. Blue Chasch, Green Chasch, and Old Chasch are similarly related, as Dirdir, and Man are biologically distinct. What does this suggest to you?''

''I agree that the circumstances are puzzling. Have you any explanation?''

''I feel that more facts are needed. Perhaps the Refluxives will become adept telepathists, and surprise us all.''

Helsse walked along in silence. They turned a corner. Reith pulled Helsse to a halt. ''Quiet!'' He waited.

The shuffle of footsteps sounded; a dark shape rounded the corner. Reith seized the figure, spun it around, applied an arm and neck lock. Helsse made one or two tentative motions; Reith trusting no one, kept him in his field of vision. ''Make a light,'' said Reith. ''Let's see whom we have. Or what.''

Helsse brought forth a glow-bulb, held it up. The captive squirmed, kicked, lurched; Reith tightened his grip and felt the snap of a bone, but the figure, sagging, toppled Reith off balance. From the unseen face came a hiss of triumph; it snatched itself free. Then, to a flicker of a metal, it gave a gasp of pain.

Helsse held up his glow-bulb, disengaged his dagger from the back of the twitching shape, while Reith stood by, mouth twisted in disapproval. ''You are quick with your blade.''

Helsse shrugged. ''His kind carry stings.'' He turned the body over with his foot; a small tinkle sounded as a glass sliver fell against the stone.

The two peered curiously into the white face, half-shrouded under the brim of an extravagantly wide black hat.

''He hats himself like a Pnumekin,'' said Helsse, ''and he is pale as a ghost.''

''Or a Wankhman,'' said Reith.

''But I think he is something different from either; what, I could not say. Perhaps a hybrid, a mingling, which, so it is said, makes the best personnel for spy work.''

Reith dislodged the hat, to reveal a stark bald pate. The face was fine-boned, somewhat loosely muscled; the nose was thin and limber and terminated in a lump. The eyes, half-open, seemed to be black. Bending close, Reith thought that the scalp had been shaven.

Helsse looked uneasily up and down the street. "Come, we must hurry away, before the patrol finds us and issues an information."

"Not so fast," said Reith. "No one is near. Hold the light; stand yonder, where you can see along the street." Helsse reluctantly obeyed and Reith was able to watch him sidelong as he searched the corpse. The garments had a queer musky odor; Reith's stomach jerked as he felt here and there. From an inner pocket of the cloak he took a clip of papers. At the belt hung a soft leather pouch, which he detached.

"Come!" hissed Helsse. "We must not be discovered, we would lose all 'place.' "

They proceeded back to the Oval and across to the Travelers' Inn. In the arcade before the entrance they paused. "The evening was interesting," said Reith. "I learned a great deal."

"I wish I could say the same," said Helsse. "What did you take from the dead man?"

Reith displayed the pouch, which contained a handful of sequins. He brought forth the clip of papers, and the two examined it in the light streaming out of the inn, to find rows of a peculiar writing: a series of rectangles, variously shaded and marked.

Helsse looked at Reith. "Do you recognize this script?"

"No."

Helsse gave a short sharp bark of laughter. "It is Wankh."

"Hm. What would be the significance of this?"

"Simply more mystery. Settra is a hive of intrigue. Spies are everywhere."

"And spy devices? Microphones? Eye-cells?"

"It is safe to assume as much."

"Then it would be safe to assume that the Refluxives' hall is monitored. . . . Perhaps I was too free with advice."

"If the dead man were the monitor, your words are now

lost. But allow me to take custody of the notes. I will have them translated; there is a colony of Lokhars nearby and some of them have a smattering of Wankh.''

''We will go together,'' said Reith. ''Will tomorrow suit you?''

''Well enough,'' said Helsse glumly. He looked off across the Oval. ''Finally then: what must I tell Lord Cizante as to the boon?''

''I don't know,'' said Reith. ''I'll have an answer tomorrow.''

''The situation may be clarified even sooner,'' said Helsse. ''here is Dordolio.''

Reith swung around, to find Dordolio striding toward him, followed by two suave cavaliers. Dordolio was clearly in a fury. He halted a yard in front of Reith and, thrusting forth his head, blurted: ''With your vicious tricks, you have ruined me! Have you no shame?'' He took off his hat, hurled it into Reith's face. Reith stepped aside, the hat went wheeeling off into the Oval.

Dordolio shook his finger in Reith's face; Reith backed away a step. ''Your death is assured,'' bellowed Dordolio. ''But not by the honor of my sword! Low-caste assassins will drown you in cattle excrement! Twenty pariahs will drub you corpse! A cur will drag your head along the street by the tongue!''

Reith managed a painful grin. ''Cizante will arrange the same for you, at my request. It's as good a boon as any.''

''Cizante, bah! A wicked parvenu, a moping invert. Blue Jade shall be nothing; the fall of that palace will culminate the 'round'!''

Helsse came slightly forward. ''Before you enlarge upon your remarkable assertions, be advised that I represent the House of Blue Jade, and that I will be impelled to report to his Excellency Lord Cizante the substance of your comments.''

''Do not bore me with triviality!'' stormed Dordolio. He

furiously motioned to Reith. "Fetch my hat, or tomorrow expect the first of the Twelve Touches!"

"A small concession," said Reith, "if it ensures your departure." He picked up Dordolio's hat, shook it once or twice, handed it to him. "Your hat, which you threw across the square." He stepped around Dordolio, entered the foyer of the inn. Dordolio gave a somewhat subdued caw of laughter, slapped his hat against his thigh and, signaling his comrades, walked away.

In the foyer of the inn Reith asked Helsse, "What are the 'Twelve Touches'?"

"At intervals—perhaps a day, perhaps two days—an assassin will tap the victim with a twig. The twelfth touch is fatal; the man dies. By accumulated poison, by a single final dose, or by morbid suggestion, only the Assassins' Guild knows. And now I must return to Blue Jade. Lord Cizante will be interested in my report."

"What do you intend to tell him?"

Helsee only laughed. "You, the most secretive of men, asking me that! Still, Cizante will hear that you have agreed to accept a boon, that you probably will soon be departing Cath—"

"I said nothing on this!"

"It will still be an element of my report."

VIII

REITH AWOKE TO WAN SUNLIGHT SHINING THROUGH THE HEAVY amber panes of the windows. He lay on the unfamiliar couch, collecting the threads of his existence. It was difficult not to feel a profound gloom. Cath, where he had hoped to find flexibility, enlightenment, and perhaps cooperation, was hardly less harsh an environment than the Aman Steppe. It was obvious folly to dream of building a spaceboat in Settra.

Reith sat up on the couch. He had known horror, grief, disillusionment, but there had been corresponding moments of triumph and hope, even a few spasmodic instants of joy. If he were to die tomorrow—or in twelve days after twelve "touches"—he had already lived a miraculous life. Very well then, he would put his destiny to the test. Helsse had predicted his departure from Cath; Helsse had read the future, or Reith's own personality, more accurately than Reith himself.

Breakfasting with Traz and Anacho he described his adventures of the previous evening. Anacho found the circumstances perturbing. "This is an insane society, constrained by punctilio as a rotten egg is held by its shell. Whatever your aims—and sometimes I think that you are the most flamboyant lunatic of all—they will not be achieved here."

''I agree.''

''Well then,'' said Traz, ''what next?''

''What I plan is dangerous, perhaps rash folly. But I see no other alternative. I intend to ask Cizante for money; this we shall share. Then I think it best that we separate. You, Traz, might do worse than to return to Wyness, and there make a life for yourself. Perhaps Anacho will do the same. Neither of you can profit by coming with me; in fact, I guarantee the reverse.''

Anacho looked off across the square. ''Until now you have managed to survive, if precariously. I find myself curious as to what you hope to achieve. With your permission, I will join your expedition, which I suspect is by no means as desperate as you make it out to be.''

''I intend to confiscate a Wankh spaceship from the Ao Hidis spaceport, or elsewhere, if it seems more convenient.''

Anacho threw his hands in the air. ''I feared no less.'' He proceeded to state a hundred objections which Reith did not trouble to contradict. ''All very true; I will end my days in a Wankh dungeon or a nighthound's belly; still this is what I intend to attempt. I strongly urge that you and Traz make your way to the Isles of Cloud and live as best you may.''

''Bah,'' snorted Anacho. ''Why won't you attempt some reasonable exploit, like exterminating the Pnume, or teaching the Chasch to sing?''

''I have other ambitions.''

''Yes, yes, your faraway planet, the home of man. I am tempted to help you, if only to demonstrate your lunacy.''

''As for me,'' said Traz, ''I would like to see this far world. I know it exists, because I saw the spaceboat in which Adam Reith arrived.''

Anacho inspected the youth with eyebrows raised. ''You have not mentioned this previously.''

''You never asked.''

''How might such an absurdity enter my mind?''

"A person who calls facts absurdities will often be surprised," said Traz.

"But at least he has organized the cosmic relationship into categories, which sets him apart from animals and sub-men."

Reith intervened. "Come now; let's put our energies to work, since you both seem bent on suicide. Today we seek information. And here is Helsse, bringing us important news, or so it appears from his aspect."

Helsse approached and gave a polite greeting. "Last night, as you may imagine, I had much to report to Lord Cizante. He urges that you make some reasonable request, which he will be glad to fulfill. He recommends that we destroy the papers taken from the spy and I am inclined to agree. If you acquiesce, Lord Cizante may grant further concessions."

"Of what nature?"

"He does not specify, but I suspect he has in mind a certain slackening of protocol in regard to your presence in Blue Jade Palace."

"I am more interested in the documents than in Lord Cizante. If he wants to see me he can come here to the inn."

Helsse gave a brittle chuckle. "Your response is no surprise. If you are ready I will conduct you to South Ebron where we fill find a Lokhar."

"There are no Yao scholars who read the Wankh language?"

"Such facility would seem pointless expertise."

"Until someone wanted a document translated."

Helsse gave an indifferent twitch. "At this play of the 'round,' Utilitarianism is an alien philosophy. Lord Cizante, for instance, would find your arguments not only incomprehensible but disgusting."

"We shall never argue the matter," said Reith equably.

Helsse had come in an extremely elegant equipage: a blue carriage with six scarlet wheels and a profusion of golden festoons. The interior was like a luxurious drawing room, with gray-green wainscoting, a pale gray carpet, an arched ceiling covered with green silk. The chairs were deeply upholstered; to the side, under windows of pale green glass, a buffet offered trays of sweetmeats. Helsse ushered his guests into the car with the utmost politeness; today he wore a suit of pale green and gray, as if to blend himself into the decor of the carriage.

When all were seated, he touched a button to close the door and retract the steps. Reith observed, ''Lord Cizanthe, while deriding utilitarianism as a doctrine, apparently does not flout its applications.''

''You refer to the door-closing mechanism? He is not aware that it exists. Someone is always at hand to touch the button for him. Like others of his class he touches objects only in play or pleasure. You find this odd? No matter. You must accept the Yao gentry as you find them.''

''Evidently you do not regard yourself as a member of the Yao gentry.''

Helsse laughed. ''More tactful might be the conjecture that I enjoy what I am doing.'' He spoke into a mesh. ''To the South Ebron Mercade.''

The carriage eased into motion. Helsse poured goblets of syrup and proffered sweetmeats. ''You are about to visit our commercial district: the source of our wealth, in fact, though it is considered vulgar to discuss it.''

''Strange,'' mused Anacho. ''Dirdir, at the highest level, are never so hoity-toity.''

''They are a different race,'' said Helsse. ''Superior? I am not convinced. The Wankh would never agree, should they trouble to examine the concept.''

Anacho gave a contemptuous shrug but said no more.

The carriage rolled through a market area: the Mercade, then into a district of small dwellings, in a wonderful diversity of style. At a cluster of squat brick towers the carriage halted. Helsse pointed to a nearby garden where sat a dozen men of spectacular appearance. They wore white shirts and trousers, their hair, long and abundant, was also white, in striking contrast to the lusterless black of their skins. ''Lokhars,'' said Helsse. "Migrating mechanics from the highlands north of Lake Falas in Central Kislovan. That is not their natural coloration; they bleach their hair and dye their skin. Some say the Wankh enforced the custom upon them thousands of years ago to differentiate them from Wankhmen, who of course are white-skinned and black-haired. In any event, they come and go, working where they gain the highest return, for they are a remarkably avaricious folk. Some, after laboring in the Wankh shops, have migrated north to Cath; a few of these know a chime or two of Wankh-talk and occasionally can puzzle out the sense of Wankh documents. Notice the old man yonder playing with the child; he is reckoned as adept in Wankh as any. He will demand a large sum for his efforts, and in order to forestall even more exorbitant demands in the future I must haggle with him. If you will be good enough to wait I will go to make the arrangements."

"A moment," said Reith. "At a conscious level I am convinced of your integrity, but I can't control my instinctive suspicions. Let us make the arrangements together."

"As you wish," said Helsse graciously. "I will send the chauffeur for the man." He spoke into the mesh.

Anacho murmured, "If the arrangements were already made, the qualms of a trusting person might easily be drugged."

Helsse nodded judiciously. "I believe I can assuage your anxieties."

A moment later the old man sauntered up to the carriage.

"Inside, if you please," said Helsse.

The old man poked his white-maned face through the door. "My time is valuable; what do you want of me?"

"A matter for your profit."

"Profit, eh? I can at least listen." He entered the carriage, and seated himself with a comfortable grunt. The air took on the odor of a spicy, slightly rancid pomade. Helsse stood in front of him. With a side glance toward Reith he said, "Our arrangement is canceled. Do not heed my instructions."

F.W. HAGOPIAN ©'86

" 'Arrangement'? 'Instructions'? What are you talking about? You must mistake me for another. I am Zarfo Detwiler."

Helsse made an easy gesture. "It's all one. We want you to translate a Wankh document for us, the guide to a treasure hoard. Translate correctly, you shall share the booty."

"No, no, none of that." Zarfo Detwiler waved a black finger. "I'll share the booty with pleasure; additionally I want a hundred sequins, and no recriminations if I fail to satisfy you."

"No recriminations, agreed. But a hundred sequins for possibly nothing? Ridiculous. Here: five sequins and eat your fill of the expensive sweetmeats."

"That last I'll do anyway; am I not your invited guest?" Zarfo Detwiler popped a handful of dainties into his mouth. "You must think me a moon-calf to offer but five sequins. Only three persons in Settra can so much as tell you which side of a Wankh ideogram is up. I alone can read meaning, by virtue of thirty toilsome years in the Ao Hidis machine shops."

The haggling proceeded; Zarfo Detwiler eventually agreed to fifty sequins and a tenth share of the assumptive spoils. Helsse signaled Reith, who produced the documents.

Zarfo Detwiler took the papers, squinted, frowned, ran his fingers through his white mane. He looked up and spoke somewhat ponderously: "I will instruct you in Wankh communication at no charge. The Wankh are a peculiar folk, totally unique. Their brain works in pulses. They see in pulses and think in pulses. Their speech comes in a pulse, a chime of many vibrations which carries all the meaning of a sentence. Each ideogram is equivalent to a chime, which is to say, a whole unit of meaning. For this reason, to read Wankh is as much a matter of divination as logic; one must enunciate an entire meaning with each ideogram. Even the Wankhmen are not always accurate. Now this matter you have here—let me see. This first chime—hm. Notice this comb? It usually signifies an equivalence, an identity. A square of this texture shading off to the right sometimes means 'truth' or 'verified perception' or 'situation' or perhaps 'present condition of the cosmos.' These marks—I don't know. This bit of shading—I think it's a person talking. Since it's at the bottom, the base tone in the chord, it would seem that—yes, this trifle here indicates positive volition. These marks—hm. Yes, these are organizers, which specify the order and emphasis of the other elements. I can't understand them; I can only guess at the total sense. Something like 'I wish to report that conditions are identical or unchanged' or 'A person is anxious to specify that the cosmos is stable.' Something of the sort. Are you sure that this is information regarding treasure?''

''It was sold to us on this basis.''

''Hm.'' Zarfo pulled at his long black nose. ''Let me see. This second symbol: notice this shading and this bit of an angle? One is 'vision'; the other is 'negation.' I can't read the organizers, but it might mean 'blindness' or 'invisiblity' . . .''

Zarfo continued his lucubrations, poring over each ideogram, occasionally tracing out a fragment of meaning, more often confessing failure, and becoming ever more restive. ''You have been gulled,'' he said at last. ''I'm certain there is no mention of money or treasure. I believe, this is no more than a commercial report. It seems to say, as close as I can fathom: 'I wish to state that conditions are the same.' Something about peculiar wishes, or hopes, or volitions. 'I will presently see the dominant man, the leader of our group.' Something unknown. 'The leader is not helpful,' or perhaps 'stays aloof.' The leader slowly changes, or metamorphoses, to the enemy.' Or perhaps, The leader slowly changes to become like the enemy.' Change of some sort—I can't understand. 'I request more money.' Something about arrival of a newcomer or stranger 'of utmost importance.' That's about all.''

Reith thought to sense an almost imperceptible relaxation in Helsse's manner.

"No great illumination," said Helsse briskly. "Well, you have done your best. Here is your twenty sequins."

" 'Twenty sequins!' " roared Zarfo Detwiler. "The price agreed was fifty! How can I buy my bit of meadowland if I am constantly cheated?"

"Oh very well, if you choose to be niggardly."

"Niggardly, indeed! Next time read the message yourself."

"I could do as well, for all the help you've given us."

"You were duped. That is no guide to treasure."

"Apparently not. Well then, good day to you."

Reith followed Zarfo from the carriage. He looked back in at Helsse. "I'll remain here, for a word or two with this gentleman."

Helsse was not pleased. "We must discuss another matter. It is necessary that the Blue Jade Lord receives information."

"This afternoon I will have a definite answer for you."

Helsse gave a curt nod. "As you wish."

The carriage departed, leaving Reith and the Lokhar standing in the street. Reith said, "Is there a tavern nearby? Perhaps we can chat over a bottle."

"I am a Lokhar," snorted the black-skinned old man. "I do not addle my brains and drain my pockets with drink; not before noon, at any rate. However you may buy me a fine Zam sausage, or a clut of head-cheese."

"With pleasure."

Zarfo led the way to a food shop; the two men took their purchases to a table on the street.

"I am amazed by your ability to read the ideograms," said Reith. "Where did you learn?"

"At Ao Hidis. I worked as a die cutter beside an old Lokhar who was a true genius. He taught me to recognize a few chimes, and showed me where the shadings matched intensity vibrations, where sonority equated with shape, where the various chord components matched texture and gradation. Both the chimes and the ideograms are regular and rational, once the eye and the ear are tuned. But the tuning is difficult.'' Zarfo took a great bite of sausage. ''Needless to say, the Wankhmen discourage such learning; if they suspect a Lokhar of diligent study, he is discharged. Oh, they are a crafty lot! They jealously guard their role as intercessors between the Wankh and the world of men. A devious folk! Their women are strangely beautiful, like black pearls, but cruel and cold, and not prone to dalliance.''

''The Wankh pay well?''

''Like everyone else, as little as possible. But we are forced to concede. If labor costs rose, they would take slaves, or train Blacks or Purples, one or the other. We would then lose employment and perhaps our freedom as well. So we strive without too much complaint, and seek more profitable employment elsewhere once we are skilled.''

''It is highly likely,'' said Reith, ''that the Yao Helsse, in the gray and green suit, will ask what we discussed. He may even offer you money.''

Zarfo bit off a chunk of sausage. ''I shall naturally tell all, if I am paid enough.''

''In that case,'' said Reith, ''our conversation must deal in pleasantries, profitless to both of us.''

Zarfo chewed thoughtfully. ''How much profit had you in mind?''

''I don't care to specify, since you would only ask Helsse for more, or try to extract the same from both of us.''

Zarfo sighed dismally. ''You have a sorry opinion of the Lokhar. Our word is our bond; once we strike a bargain we do not deviate.''

The haggling continued on a more or less cordial level until for the sum of twenty sequins Zarfo agreed to guard the privacy of the conversation as fiercely as he might the hiding place of his money, and the sum was paid over.

''Back to the Wankh message for a moment,'' said Reith. ''There were references to a 'leader.' Were there hints or clues by which to identify him!''

Zarfo pursed his lips. ''A wolf-tone indicating high-level

gentry; another honorific brevet which might signify something like 'a person of the excellent sort' or 'in your own image,' 'of your sort.' It is very difficult. A Wankh reading the ideogram would understand a chime, which then would stimulate a visual image complete in essential details. The Wankh would be furnished a mental image of the person, but for someone like myself there are only crude outlines. I can tell you no more."

"You work in Settra?"

"Alas. A man of my years and impoverished: isn't it a pity? But I near my goal, and then—back to Smargash, in Lokhara, for a bit of meadow, a young wife, a comfortable chair by the hearth."

"You worked in the space shops at Ao Hidis?"

"Yes indeed; I transferred from the tool works to the space shops, where I repaired and installed air purifiers."

"Lokhar mechanics must be very skillful, then."

"Oh, indeed."

"Certain mechanics specialize upon the installation of, say, controls and instruments?"

"Naturally. Complex trades, both."

"Have such mechanics immigrated to Settra?"

Zarfo gave Reith a calculating glance. "How much is the information worth to you?"

"Control your avarice," said Reith. "No more money today. Another sausage, if you like."

"Later, perhaps. Now as to the mechanics: in Smargash are dozens, hundreds, retired after lifetimes of toil."

"Could they be tempted to join in a dangerous venture?"

"No doubt, if the danger were scant and the profit high. What do you propose?"

Reith threw caution to the winds. "Assume that someone wished to confiscate a Wankh spaceship and fly it to an unspecified destination: how many specialists would be required, and how much would it cost to hire them?"

Zarfo, to Reith's relief, did not stare in bewilderment or

shock. He gnawed for a moment at the last of the sausage. Then, after a belch, he said, "I believe that you are asking if I consider the exploit feasible. It has often been discussed in a jocular manner, and for a fact the ships are not stringently guarded. The project is feasible. But why should you want a spaceship? I do not care to visit the Dirdir on Sibol or test the infinity of the universe."

"I can't discuss the destination."

"Well then, how much money do you offer?"

"My plans have not progressed to that stage. What do you consider a suitable fee?"

"To risk life and freedom? I would not stir for less than fifty thousand sequins."

Reith rose to his feet. "You have your fifty sequins; I have my information. I trust you to keep my secret."

Zarfo sat sprawled back in his chair. "Now then, not so fast. After all I am old and my life is not worth so much after all. Thirty thousand? Twenty? Ten?"

"The figure starts to become practical. How much of a crew will we need?"

"Four or five more, possibly six. You envision a long voyage?"

"As soon as we are in space, I will reveal our destination. Ten thousand sequins is only a preliminary payment. Those who go with me will return with wealth beyond their dreams."

Zarfo rose to his feet. "When do you propose to leave?"

"As soon as possible. Another matter: Settra is overrun with spies; it's important that we attract no attention."

Zarfo gave a hoarse laugh. "So this morning you approach me in a vast carriage, worth thousands of sequins. A man watches us even now."

"I've been noticing him. But he seems too obvious to be a spy. Well, then, where shall we meet, and when?"

"Upon the stroke of midmorning tomorrow, at the stall of Upas the spice merchant in the Cercade. Be certain you are not followed. . . . That fellow yonder I believe to be an assassin, from the style of his garments.''

The man at this moment approached their table. ''You are Adam Reith?''

''Yes.''

''I regret to say that the Security Assassination Company has accepted a contract made out in your name: the Death of the Twelve Touches. I will now administer the first innoculation. Will you be so good as to bare your arm? I will merely prick you with this splint.''

Reith backed away. ''I'll do nothing of the sort.''

''Depart!'' Zarfo Detwiler told the assassin. ''This man is worth ten thousand sequins to me alive; dead, nothing.''

The assassin ignored Zarfo. To Reith he said, ''Please do not make an undignified display. The process then becomes protracted and painful for us all. So then—''

Zarfo roared: ''Stand away; have I not warned you?'' He snatched up a chair and struck the assassin to the ground. Zarfo was not yet satisfied. He picked up the splint, jabbed it into the back of the man's thigh, through the rust-ocher corduroy of his trousers. ''Halt!'' wailed the assassin. ''That is Innoculation Number One!''

Zarfo seized a handful of splints from the splayed-open wallet. ''And here,'' he roared, ''are numbers Two to Twelve!'' And with a foot on the man's neck he thrust the handful into the twitching buttocks. ''There you are, you knave! Do you want the next episode, Numbers Thirteen to Twenty-four?''

''No, no, let me be; I am a dead man now!''

''If not, you're a cheat as well as an assassin!''

Passersby had halted to watch. A portly woman in pink silk rushed forward. ''You hairy black villain, what are you doing to that poor assassin? He is only a workman at his trade!''

Zarfo picked up the assassin's work sheet, looked down the list. ''Hm. It appears that your husband is next on his list.''

The woman looked with startled eyes after the assassin now tottering off down the street.

"Time we were leaving," said Reith.

They walked through back alleys to a small shed, screened from the street by a lattice of woven withe. "It is the neighborhood corpse-house," said Zarfo. "No one will bother us here."

Reith entered, looked gingerly around the stone benches on one of which lay the hulk of a small animal.

"Now when," said Zarfo, "who is your enemy?"

"I suspect a certain Dordolio," said Reith. "I can't be sure."

Zarfo scrutinized the work sheet. "Well, we shall see. 'Adam Reith, the Travelers' Inn—Contract Number Two-three-o-five, Style Eighteen; prepaid.' Dated today, surcharged 'Rush.' Prepaid, eh? Well then, let us try a ruse. Back to my cottage."

He took Reith to one of the brick towers, entered by an arched doorway. On a table rested a telephone. Zarfo lifted the instrument with cautious fingers. "Connect me with the Security Assassination Company."

A grave voice spoke. "We are here to serve your needs."

"I refer to Contract Number Two-three-o-five," said Zarfo, "relating to a certain Adam Reith. I can't find the estimate and I wish to pay the charges."

"A moment, my lord."

The voice presently returned. "The contract was prepaid, my lord; and was scheduled for execution this morning."

"Prepaid? Impossible. I did not prepay. What is the name on the receipt?"

"The name is Helsse Izam. I'm sure there is no mistake, sir."

"Perhaps not. I'll discuss the matter with the person involved."

"Thank you, sir, for your custom."

IX

REITH RETURNED TO THE TRAVELERS' INN, AND WITH A CERTAIN trepidation entered the foyer where he found Traz. "What has occurred, if anything?"

Traz, the most lucid and decisive of individuals, was less deft when it came to communicating a mood. "The Yao—Helsse, is that his name?—became silent after you left the carriage. Perhaps he found us strange company. He told us that tonight we would dine with the Blue Jade Lord, that he would come early to instruct us in decorum. Then he drove off in the carriage."

A perplexing sequence of events, reflected Reith. An interesting point: the contract had specified Twelve Touches. If his death were urgently required, a knife, a bullet, an energy bolt would serve the purpose. But the first of twelve injections? A device to stimulate haste?

"Many things are happening," he told Traz. "Events I don't pretend to understand."

"The sooner we leave Settra the better," gloomed Traz.

"Agreed."

Anacho the Dirdirman appeared, freshly barbered and splendid in a new high-collared black jacket, pale blue trousers, scarlet ankle-high slippers with modish upturned toes. Reith took the two to a secluded alcove and described the events of the day. ''So now we need only money, which I hope to extract from Cizante tonight.''

The hours of the afternoon passed slowly. At last Helsse appeared, wearing a modish suit of canary yellow velvet. He gave polite greetings to the group. ''You are enjoying your visit to Cath?''

''Indeed yes,'' said Reith. ''I have never felt so relaxed.''

Helsse maintained his aplomb. ''Excellent. Now, in regard to this evening, Lord Cizante suspects that you and your friends might find a formal dinner somewhat tedious. He recommends rather a casual and unstructured tiffin, at a time to suit your convenience: now, if you so desire.''

''We are ready,'' said Reith. ''But, to anticipate any misunderstanding, please remember that we insist upon a dignified reception. We do not intend to slink into the palace by a back entrance.''

Helsse made an easy gesture. ''For a casual occasion, casual protocol. That's our rule.''

''I will be specific,'' said Reith. ''Our 'place' demands that we use the front entrance. If Lord Cizante objects, then he must meet us elsewhere: perhaps at the tavern around the Oval.''

Helsse uttered an incredulous laugh. ''He would as soon don a buffoon's cap and cut capers in Merrymakers' Round!'' He shook his head dolefully. ''To avoid difficulties we will use the front entrance; after all what difference does it make?''

Reith laughed. ''Especially since Cizante has ordered us brought in by the scullery and will assume that this is how we entered. . . . Well, it's a fair compromise. Let's go.''

The trip to Blue Jade Palace was made in a sleek black landau. At Helsse's instructions it drove up to the formal portal. Helsse alighted, and with a thoughtful glance along the façade of the palace, conducted the three outlanders through the main portal and into the great foyer. He muttered a few words to a footman, then ushered the three up a flight of shallow stairs, into a small green and gold salon overlooking the courtyard.

Lord Cizante was nowhere to be seen.

"Please be seated," said Helsse affably. "Lord Cizante will be with you shortly." He gave a jerk of the head and departed the chamber.

Several minutes passed, then Lord Cizante appeared. He wore a long white gown, white slippers, a black skullcap. His face was petulant and brooding; he looked from face to face. "Which is the man to whom I spoke before?"

Helsse muttered in his ear; he turned to face Reith. "I see. Well then, make yourself easy. Helsse, you have ordered a suitable refreshment?"

"Indeed, your Excellency."

A footman rolled in a buffet and offered trays of sweet wafers, salt-bark, cubes of spiced meat, decanters of wine, flagons of essence. Reith accepted wine; Traz a goblet of syrup. Anacho took green essences; Lord Cizante selected a stick of incense and walked back and forth, jerking it through the air. "I have negative news for you," he said abruptly. "I have decided to withdraw all proffers and undertakings. In short, you may expect no boon."

Reith sipped the wine and gave himself time to think. "You are honoring Dordolio's claim?"

"I cannot elaborate upon the matter. The statement may be interpreted in its most general sense."

"I have no claim upon you," said Reith. "I came here yesterday only to convey news of your daughter."

Lord Cizante held the incense stick under his nostrils. "The circumstances no longer interest me."

Anacho emitted a somewhat startling caw of laughter. "Understandable! To acknowledge them would force you to honor your pledge!"

"Not at all," said Lord Cizante. "I spoke only for the attention of Blue Jade personnel."

"Ha ha! Who will believe that, now that you have hired assassins against my friend?"

Lord Cizante held the incense still and poised. "Assassins? What of this?"

"Your aide"—Reith indicated Helsse—"took out a Type Eighteen contract against me. I intend to warn Dordolio; your penury carries a vicious sting."

Lord Cizante turned a frowning glance upon Helsse. "What of this?"

Helsse stood with black eyebrows fretfully raised. "I endeavored only to fulfill my function."

"Misplaced zeal! Would you make Blue Jade a laughing stock? If this sordid tale gains circulation . . ." His voice suddenly trailed off. Helsse gave a shrug, and poured himself a goblet of wine.

Reith rose to his feet. "Our business appears to be at an end."

"A moment," said Lord Cizante curtly. "Let me consider. . . . You realize that this so-called assassination is a mare's-nest?"

Reith slowly shook his head. "You have blown hot and cold too often; I am totally skeptical."

Lord Cizante swung on his heel. The incense stick fell to the rug, where it began to smolder. Reith picked it up, placed it on the tray. "Why do you do that?" asked Helsse in sardonic wonder.

"You must supply your own answer."

Lord Cizante strode back into the room. He gestured to Helsse, took him into the corner, muttered a moment, and once again departed.

Helsse turned to Reith. "Lord Cizante has empowered me to pay over to you a sum of ten thousand sequins on condition that you depart Cath instantly, returning to Kotan by the first cog out of Vervodei."

"Lord Cizante's impertinence is amazing," said Reith.

Anacho asked casually, "How high will he go?"

"He specified no precise sum," Helsse admitted. "He is interested only in your departure, which he will facilitate in every detail."

"A million sequins, then," said Anacho. "If we must acquiesce to this undignified scheme, we might as well sell ourselves dear."

"Much too dear," said Helsse. "Twenty thousand sequins is more reasonable."

"Not reasonable enough," said Reith. "We need more, much more."

Helsse surveyed the three in silence. He said at last: "To avoid wasting time I will announce the maximum sum Lord Cizante cares to pay. It is fifty thousand sequins, which I personally consider generous, and transportation to Vervodei."

"We accept," said Reith. "Needless to say, you must cancel the contract with the Security Company."

Helsse smiled a small tremulous smile. "I have already received my instructions in this regard. And when will you depart Settra?"

"In a day or so."

With fifty strips of purple-celled sequins, the three left Blue Jade Palace, and climbed into the waiting black landau. Helsse did not accompany them.

The landau wheeled east through the cinnamon dusk, under luminants which as yet cast no illumination. Off in the parks, palaces and town houses showed clusters of blurred lights, and in one great garden a fête was in progress.

The landau rumbled across a carved wooden bridge hung with lanterns, to enter a district of crowded timber buildings, with tearooms and cafés jutting over the street. They passed through an area of bleak half-deserted tenements, and at last came into the Oval.

Reith descended from the landau. Traz sprang past and

threw himself on a dark silent figure. At the glint of metal Reith ducked to the ground, but failed to escape a violent purple-white flash. A hot blow pounded his head; he lay half-stunned, while Traz struggled with the assailant. Anacho stepped forward, pointed his sting. Out sprang the thin shaft, piercing the man's shoulder. The gun clattered to the cobbles.

Reith picked himself up, stood weaving. The side of his head smarted as if by a scald; the smell of ozone and burnt hair filled his nostrils. He tottered over to where Traz held the hooded figure in an armlock while Anacho removed his wallet and dagger. The man wore a half-hood; Reith raised it, revealing, to his astonishment, the face of the Yearning Refluxive to whom he had spoken the night before.

People here and there about the Oval, at first cautious of the struggle, now started to approach. There came the shrill hoot of the patrol whistle. The Refluxive struggled to free himself. "Release me; they'll make me a terrible example!"

"Why did you try to kill me?" demanded Reith.

"Need you ask? Let me go, I beg you!"

"Why should I? You just tried to murder me! Let them take you."

"No! The association will suffer!"

"Well then—why did you try to kill me?"

"Because you are dangerous! You would divide us! Already there is dissension! A few weak souls have no faith; they want to find a spaceship and go off on a journey! Folly! The only way is the orthodox way! You are a danger; I thought it best to expunge your dissidence."

Reith took a deep breath of exasperation. The patrol was almost upon them. He said: "Tomorrow we leave Settra; you've had your trouble for nothing!" He gave the man a shove which sent him staggering and crying for the pain in his shoulder. "Be thankful we are merciful men!"

The Refluxive disappeared in the darkness. The patrol ran up: tall men in striped suits of red and black holding staffs terminating in incandescent tips. "What is the trouble?"

"A thief," said Reith. "He tried to rob us, then ran off behind the buildings."

The patrol departed; Reith, Anacho, and Traz went into the inn. As they supped Reith told of his arrangements with Zarfo Detwiler. "Tomorrow, if all goes well, we depart Settra."

"By no means too soon," remarked Anacho sourly.

"True. Already I've been spied on by the Wankh, persecuted by the gentry, shot at by the 'cult.' My nerves won't allow much more."

A boy wearing dark red livery came up to their table. "Adam Reith?"

"Who wants him?" Reith asked warily.

"I have a message."

"Give it here." Reith tore apart the folded paper, puzzled out the sense of the florid symbols:

The Security Company sends greetings. Be it known that, since you, Adam Reith, have attacked an authorized employee in the innocent pursuit of his duties, spoiling his equipment and inflicting pain and inconvenience, we demand a retributive fee of eighteen thousand sequins. If the sum is not *immediately paid at our main office, you will be killed by a combination of several processes. Your prompt cooperation will be appreciated. Please do not depart Settra or seek to deny us in any way, as in that case the penalties must be amplified.*

Reith flung the letter down on the table. "Dordolio, the Wankh, Lord Cizante, and Hellse, the 'cult,' the Security Company: who is left?"

Traz commented: "Tomorrow may hardly be soon enough."

X

THE FOLLOWING MORNING REITH COMMUNICATED WITH BLUE Jade Palace by means of the queer Yao telephones, and was allowed to speak to Helsse. "You have naturally canceled the contract with the Security Company?"

"The contract has been canceled. I understand that they have decided to take independent action, which of course you must deal with as you see fit."

"Exactly," said Reith. "We are leaving Settra at once and we accept Lord Cizante's offer of assistance."

Helsse made a noncommittal sound. "What are your plans?"

"Essentially, to escape Settra with our lives."

"I will arrive shortly and take you to an outlying wheelway station. At Vervodei ships leave daily for all quarters and no doubt you will be able to make a convenient departure."

"We will be ready at noon, or before."

Reith set out on foot for the Cercade, taking all precautions, and arrived at the rendezvous with fair assurance that he had not been followed. Zarfo stood waiting, his white hair confined in a bonnet as black as his face. He immediately led the way to the cellar of an ale house. They sat at a stone table; Zarfo signaled the pot-boy and they were presently served heavy stone mugs of a bitter earthy ale.

P.W.HAGOPIAN ©'86

Zarfo came quickly to business. ''Before I disrupt my life by so much as a twitch, show me the color of your money.''

Without words Reith threw down ten strips of winking purple sequins.

''Aha!'' gloated Zarfo Detwiler. ''This is true beauty! Is it to be mine? I will take custody of it at once, and guard it from all harm.''

''Who will guard you?'' asked Reith.

''Tish tush, lad,'' scoffed Zarfo. ''If comrades can't trust comrades in a cool ale-cellar, how will it go under adversity?''

Reith returned the money to his wallet. ''Adversity is here now. The assassins are disturbed by the affair of yesterday. Instead of taking revenge upon you, they have threatened me.''

''Yes, they are an unreasonable lot. If they demand money, defy them. A man can always fight for his life.''

''I've been warned not to leave Settra until such a time as they choose to kill me. Nevertheless, I propose to depart, and as soon as possible.''

''Shrewd.'' Zarfo quaffed ale and set the mug down with a thud. ''But how will you evade the assassins? Naturally they ponder your every move.''

Reith jerked around at a noise, only to find the pot-boy at hand to refill Zarfo's mug. Zarfo pulled at his long black nose to conceal a grin. ''The assassins are pertinacious, but we shall outwit them, one way or another. Return to your hotel and make all ready. At noon I will join you and we shall see what we shall see.''

''Noon? So late?''

''What difference an hour or two? I must wind up my affairs.''

Reith returned to the inn, where Helsse had already arrived in the black landau. The atmosphere was strained and taut; at the sight of Reith, Helsse jumped to his feet. ''Time is short; we have been waiting! Come; we have only enough time to catch the first afternoon car for Vervodei!''

Reith asked: "Won't the assassins be expecting just this? It seems an unimaginative plan."

Helsse gave an irritable shrug. "Do you have a better idea?"

"I'd like to work one out."

Anacho asked, "Does Lord Cizante keep an air-car?"

"It is not in operation."

"Are any others available?"

"For a purpose of this sort? I should think not."

Five minutes passed. Helsse said mildly, "The longer we wait, the less time remains to you." He pointed out the window. "See the two men in the round hats? They wait for you to come forth. Now we cannot even use the car."

"Go out and tell them to go away," suggested Reith.

Helsse laughed. "Not I."

Another half an hour went by. Zarfo swaggered into the foyer. He saluted the group with a wave of the hand. "Are all ready?"

Reith pointed to the assassins standing to the side of the Oval. "They are waiting for us."

"Detestable creatures," said Zarfo. "Only in Cath would they be tolerated." He looked sidelong at Helsse. "Why is he here?"

Reith explained the circumstances; Zarfo looked out upon the Oval. "The black car with the silver and blue crest—is that the vehicle in question? If so, nothing is simpler. We shall ride off in the car."

"Not feasible," said Helsse.

"Why not?" asked Reith.

"Lord Cizante does not care to become involved in this matter, nor do I. At the very least, the Company would include me in the contract."

Reith laughed bitterly. "When you contracted with them in the first place? Out to the car, and drive us away from this city of madmen!"

After a moment of incredulous disdain, Helsse gave a curt nod. "As you wish."

The group left the inn and walked to the car. The assassins came forward. "I believe that you, sir, are Adam Reith?"

"What of it?"

"May we inquire your destination?"

"The Blue Jade Palace."

"Correct," said Helsse tonelessly.

"You understand our regulations and schedule of penalties?"

"Yes, of course."

The assassins muttered together, then one said: "In this case we think it advisable to accompany you."

"There is no room," said Helsse in a cool voice.

The assassins paid no heed. One started to enter the landau. Zarfo pulled him back. The assassin looked over his shoulder. "Have a care; I am a guildsman."

"And I am a Lokhar." Zarfo struck him a great clout, sending him sprawling. The second assassin stood astounded, then snatched forth a gun. Anacho's sting snapped forth, to penetrate his chest. The first assassin tried to crawl away; Zarfo gave him a tremendous kick under the chin; he fell flat and limp. "Into the car," said Zarfo. "It is time to leave."

"What a fiasco," whispered Helsse. "I am ruined."

"Away from Settra!" cried Zarfo. "By the least obvious route!"

The landau rolled along narrow streets, into a narrow lane, and presently out into the countryside.

"Where are you taking us?" demanded Reith.

"Vervodei."

"Ridiculous!" snorted Zarfo. "Drive east into the back country. We must make our way to the Jinga River and face downstream to Kabasas on the Parapan."

Helsse tried a voice of calm reason. "To the east is wilderness. The car will stop. We have no spare energy cells."

"No difference!"

"Not to you. But how will I return to Settra?"

"Is this your plan, after what has happened?"

Helsse muttered something under his breath. "I am a marked man. They will demand fifty thousand sequins, which I cannot pay—all through your insane manipulations."

"Whatever you like. But continue east, until the car stops or the road gives out—whichever first."

Helsse made a gesture of fateful despair.

The road led through a weirdly beautiful flatland with slow streams and ponds to either side. Trees with drooping black limbs trailed tobacco-brown foliage into the water. Reith kept a lookout to the rear, but discovered no sign of pursuit. Settra became one with the murk of distance.

Helsse no longer seemed to be sulking, but watched the road ahead with an expression that almost seemed anticipation. Reith became suddenly suspicious. "Stop a moment!"

Helsse looked around. "Stop? Why?"

"What lies ahead?"

"The mountains."

"Why is the road in such good repair? There seems to be no great traffic."

"Ho!" crowed Zarfo. "The mountain camp for insane folk! It must lie ahead!"

Helsse contrived a sickly grin. "You told me to drive you to the end of road; you did not stipulate that I should avoid taking you to the asylum."

"I do so now," said Reith. "Please, no more innocent errors of this sort."

Helsse compressed his lips and once more began to brood. At a crossroad he swung south. The ground began to rise. Reith asked, '"Where does the road lead?"

"To the old quicksilver mines, to mountain retreats, a few peasant holdings."

Into a forest hung with black moss rolled the car, and the road slanted up ever more steeply. The sun passed behind a cloud, the forest became dark and dank, then gave way to a foggy meadow.

Helsse glanced at an indicator. "An hour more of energy."

Reith indicated the thrust of mountains ahead. "What lies beyond?"

"Wilderness. The Hoch Har tribes, Black Mountain Lake, source of the Jinga. The route is neither safe nor convenient. It is, however, an exit from Cath."

Across the meadow they drove. Thick-trunked trees rose at intervals with leaves like shelves of yellow fungus.

The road began to fail, and in places was blocked by fallen boughs. The ridge loomed above, a great rocky jut.

At an abandoned mine the road ended. Simultaneously the power index reached zero. The car halted with a thud and a bump; there was silence except for a sigh of wind.

The group alighted with their meager possessions. The fog had dissipated; the sun shone cool through a high overcast, washing the landscape in honey-colored light.

Reith surveyed the mountainside, tracing a path to the ridge. He turned to Helsse. "Well, which is it to be?" Kabasas, or back to Settra?"

"Settra, naturally." He looked disconsolately at the car.

"Afoot?"

"Better than afoot to Kabasas."

"What of the assassins?"

"I must take my chances."

Reith brought out his scanscope and studied the way they had come. "There seems no sign of pursuit; you—" He halted, surprised by the expression on Helsse's face.

"What is that object?" demanded Helsse.

Reith explained.

"Dordolio spoke accurately," said Helsse in a wondering voice. "He was telling the truth!"

Half-amused, half-annoyed, Reith said, "I don't know what Dordolio told you, other than that we were barbarians. Good-bye, then, and my regards to Lord Cizante."

''Wait a moment,'' said Helsse, staring indecisively west toward Settra. ''Kabasas may be safer, after all. The assassins would be sure to consider me an auxiliary to your offense.'' He turned, assessed the bulk of the mountain, heaved a gloomy sigh. ''Total insanity, of course.''

''Needless to say, we are not here by our own volition,'' returned Reith. ''Well, we might as well start.''

They climbed the tailings dump in front of the mine, peered into the tunnel, from which issued an ooze of reddish slime. A set of footprints led into the tunnel. They were about human size, the shape of a bowling pin or a gourd; two inches ahead of the narrow forward end was three indentations as of toes. Looking down at the marks Reith felt the hairs rise at the nape of his neck. He listened, but no sounds came from the tunnel. He asked Traz, ''What sort of prints are these?''

''An unshod Phung, possibly—a small one. More likely a Pnume. The prints are fresh. It watched our approach.''

''Come along; let's leave,'' muttered Reith.

An hour later they reached the ridge and halted to gaze out over the panorama. The land to the west lay drowned in late afternoon murk, with Settra showing as a discolored spot, like a bruise. Far to the east glimmered Black Mountain Lake.

The travelers spent an eerie night at the edge of a forest, starting up at far noises: a thin uncanny screaming, a rap-rap-rap, like blows against a block of hard wood, the crafty hooting of night-hounds.

Dawn came at last. The group made a glum breakfast on pods from a pilgrim plant, then proceeded down over a basalt palisade to the floor of a wooded valley. Ahead lay the Black Mountain Lake, calm and still. A fishing boat inched across the water and presently disappeared behind a jut of rock. ''Hoch Har,'' said Helsse. ''Ancient enemies of the Yao. Now they remain behind the mountains.''

Traz pointed. ''A path.''

Reith looked. ''I see no path.''

"Nevertheless it is there, and I smell wood smoke, from a distance of three miles."

Five minutes later Traz made a sudden gesture. "Several men are approaching."

Reith listened; he could hear nothing. But presently three men appeared on the trail ahead: very tall men with thick waists, thin arms and legs, wearing skirts of a dirty white fiber and short capes of the same stuff. They stopped short at the sight of the travelers, then turned and retreated along the trail, looking anxiously back over their shoulders.

After a quarter-mile the trail left the jungle, and angled off across the swampy foreshore of the lake. The Hoch Har village stood on stilts over the water, with a dock extending a hundred yards out over the water, terminating in a float to which a dozen plank boats were tied. On the shore a score of men stood in attitudes of nervous truculence, striding back and forth, bush-knives and long spring-bows at the ready.

The travelers approached.

The tallest and heaviest of the Hoch Hars called out in a ridiculously shrill voice: "Who are you?"

"Travelers on the way to Kabasas."

The Hoch Hars stared incredulously, then peered back up the trail toward the mountains. "Where is the rest of your band?"

"There is no band; we are alone. Can you sell us a boat and some food?"

The Hoch Hars put aside their weapons. "Food is hard to come by," groaned the first man. "Boats are our dearest possessions. What can you offer us in exchange?"

"Only a few sequins."

"What good are sequins when we must visit Cath to spend them?"

Helsse muttered in Reith's ear. Reith said to the Hoch Hars, "Very well then, we shall continue. I understand that there are other villages around the lake."

"What? Would you deal with petty thieves and cheats? It

is all those folk are. Well, to save you from your own folly, we will strain ourselves to work out some sort of arrangement."

In the end Reith paid two hundred sequins for a boat in fair condition and what the Hoch Har chief gruffly claimed to be sufficient provisions to take them all the way to Kabasas: crates of dried fish, sacks of tubers, rolls of pepper-bark, fresh and preserved fruit. Another thirty sequins secured the services, as a guide, of a certain Tsutso, a moon-faced young man, somewhat portly, with an affable big-toothed smile. Tsutso declared the first stages of their journey to be the most precarious: "First, the rapids; then the Great Slant, after which the voyage becomes no more than drifting downstream to Kabasas."

At noon, with the small sail set, the boat departed the Hoch Har village, and through the long afternoon sailed the dark water south toward a pair of bluffs which marked the outlet of the lake and the head of the Jinga River. At sunset the boat passed between the bluffs, each crowned by a tumble of ruins, black on the brown-ash sky. Under the bluff to the right was a small cove with a beach; here Reith wanted to camp for the night but Tsutso would not hear of it. "The castles are haunted. At midnight the ghosts of old Tschai walk the pavings. Do you want us all put under a taint?"

"So long as the ghosts keep to the castle, what's to prevent us from using the cove?"

Tsutso gave Reith a wondering look, and held the boat to midstream between the opposing ruins. A mile downstream the Jinga split around a rocky islet, to which Tsutso took the boat. "Here nothing from the forest can molest us."

The travelers supped, laid themselves down around the campfire and were troubled by no more than soft whistles and trills from the forest, and once, far in the distance, the mournful call of the night-hounds.

On the next day they passed across ten miles of violent rapids, during which Tsutso ten times over earned his fee, in Reith's estimation. Meanwhile the forest dwindled to clumps of thorn; the banks became barren, and presently a strange sound made itself heard from ahead: a sibilant all-pervading roar. "The Slant," explained Tsutso. The river disappeared at a brink a hundred yards ahead. Before Reith or the others could protest, the boat had pitched over the verge.

Tsutso said, "Everyone alert; here is the Slant. Hold to the middle!"

The roar of water almost overwhelmed his voice. The boat was sliding into a dark gorge; with amazing velocity the rock walls passed astern. The river itself was a trembling black surface, lined with foam static in relation to the boat. The travelers crouched as low as possible, ignoring Tsutso's condescending grin. For minutes they dashed down the race, finally plunged into a field of foam and froth, then floated smoothly out into still water.

The walls rose sheer a thousand feet: brown sandstone pocked with balls of black starbush. Tsutso steered the boat to a fringe of shingle. "Here I leave you."

"Here? At the bottom of this canyon?" Reith asked in wonder.

Tsutso pointed to a trail winding up the slope. "Five miles away is the village."

"In that case," said Reith, "goodbye and many thanks."

Tsutso made an indulgent gesture. "It is nothing in particular. Hoch Hars are generous folk, except where the Yao are concerned. Had you been Yao, all might not have gone so well."

Reith looked toward Helsse, who said nothing. "The Yao are your enemies?"

"Our ancient persecutors, who destroyed the Hoch Har empire. Now they keep to their side of the mountain, which is well for them, as we can smell out a Yao like a bad fish." He jumped nimbly ashore. "The swamps lie ahead. Unless you lose yourselves or arouse the swamp-people you are as good as at Kabasas." With a final wave he started up the path.

* * *

The boat drifted through sepia gloom, the sky a watered silk ribbon high above. The afternoon passed, with the walls of the chasm gradually opening out. At sunset the travelers camped on a small beach, to pass a night in eerie silence.

The next day the river emerged into a wide valley overgrown with tall yellow grass. The hills retreated; the vegetation along the shore became thick and dense, and alive with small creatures half-spider, half-monkey, which whined and yelped and spurted jets of noxious fluid toward the boat. Other streams made confluence; the Jinga became broad and placid. On the following day trees of remarkable stature appeared along the shore, raising a variety of silhouettes against the smoke-brown sky, and by noon the boat floated with jungle to either side. The sail hung limp; the air was dank with odors of wet wood and decay. The hopping tree-creatures kept to the high branches; through the dimness below drifted gauze-moths, insects hanging on pale bubbles, bird-like creatures which seemed to swim on four soft wings. Once the travelers heard heavy groaning and trampling sounds, another time a ferocious hissing and again a set of strident shrieks, from sources invisible.

By slow degrees the Jinga broadened to become a placid flood, flowing around dozens of small islands, each overgrown with fronds, plumes, fan-shaped dendrons. Once, from the corner of his eye, Reith glimpsed what seemed to be a canoe carrying three youths wearing peacock-tail headdresses, but when he turned to look he saw only an island, and was never sure what in fact he had seen. Later in the day a sinuous twenty-foot beast swam after them, but fifty feet from the boat it seemed to lose interst and submerged.

At sundown the travelers made camp on the beach of a small island. Half an hour later Traz became uneasy and, nudging Reith, pointed to the underbrush. They heard a stealthy rustling and presently sensed a clammy odor. An instant later the beast which had swam after them lunged forth screaming. Reith fired one of his explosive pellets into the very maw of the beast; with its head blown off it careened in a circle, using a peculiar prancing gait, finally floundering in the water to sink.

The group gingerly resumed their seats around the campfire. Helsse watched Reith return the hand gun to his pouch, and could no longer restrain his curiosity. "Where, may I ask, did you obtain your weapon?"

"I have learned," said Reith, "that candor makes problems. Your friend Dordolio thinks me a lunatic; Anacho the Dirdirman prefers the term 'amnesiac.' So—think whatever you like."

Helsse murmured, as if for his own ears: "What strange tales we all could tell, if candor indeed were the rule."

Zarfo guffawed. "Candor? Who needs it? I'll tell strange tales as long as someone will listen."

"No doubt," said Helsse. "but persons with desperate goals must hold their secrets close."

Traz, who disliked Helsse, looked sidewise with something like a sneer. "Who could this be? I have neither secrets nor desperate goals."

"It must be the Dirdirman," said Zarfo with a sly wink.

Anacho shook his head. "Secrets? No. Only reticences. Desperate goals? I travel with Adam Reith since I have nothing better to do. I am an outcast among the sub-men. I have no goals whatever, except survival."

Zarfo said, "I have a secret: the location of my poor hoard of sequins. My goals? Equally modest: an acre or two of river meadow south of Smargash, a cabin under the tayberry trees, a polite maiden to boil my tea. I recommend them to you."

Helsse, looking into the campfire, smiled faintly. "My every thought, willy-nilly, is a secret. As for my goals—if I return to Settra and somehow can appease the Security Company, I'll be well content."

Reith looked up to where clouds were clotting out the stars. "I'll be content to stay dry tonight."

The group carried the boat ashore, turned it over and, with the sail, made a shelter. Rain began to fall, extinguishing the campfire and sending puddles of water under the boat.

Dawn finally arrived: a blear of rain and umber gloom. At noon, with the clouds breaking apart, the travelers once more floated the boat, loaded the provisions and set off to the south.

The Jinga widened until the shores were no more than dark marks. The afternoon passed; sunset was a vast chaos of black, gold, and brown. Drifting through the gloom, the travelers sought for a place to land. Mud flats lined the shore, but at last, as purple-brown dusk became night, a sandy bluff appeared under which the travelers landed for the night.

On the following day they entered the swamps. The Jinga, dividing into a dozen channels, moved sluggishly among islands of reeds, and the travelers passed a cramped night in the boat. Toward evening of the day following they came upon a canted dike of gray schist which, rising and falling, created a chain of rocky islands across the swamp. At some immensely remote time, one or another people of old Tschai had used the islands to support a causeway, long toppled to a crumble of black concrete. On the largest of the islands the travelers camped, dining on the dried fish and musty lentils provided by the Hoch Hars.

Traz was restless. He made a circuit of the island, clambered to the highest jut, looked back and forth along the line of the ancient bridge. Reith, disturbed by Traz's apprehensions, joined him. "What do you see?"

"Nothing."

Reith looked all around. The water reflected the dusky mauve of the sky, the hulks of the nearby islands. They returned to the campfire, and Reith set sentry watches. He awoke at dawn and instantly wondered why he had not been called. Then he noticed that the boat was gone. He shook

Traz, who had stood the first watch. "Last night, whom did you call?"

"Helsse."

"He did not call me. And the boat is missing."

"And Helsse as well," said Traz.

Reith saw this to be the case.

Traz pointed to the next island, forty yards across the water. "There is the boat. Helsse went for a midnight row."

Going down to the water's edge Reith called: Helsse! Helsse!"

No response. Helsse was not visible.

Reith considered the distance to the boat. The water was smooth and opaque as slate. Reith shook his head. The boat so near, so obvious: bait? From his pouch he took the hank of cord, originally a component of his survival kit, and tied a stone to one end. He heaved the stone at the boat. It fell short. Reith dragged it back through the water. For an instant the line went taut and quivered to the presence of something strong and vital.

Reith grimaced. He heaved the stone again, and now it wedged inside the boat. He pulled; the boat came back across the water.

With Traz, Reith returned to the neighboring island, to find no trace of Helsse. But under a jut of rock they found a hole slanting down into the island. Traz put his head close to the opening, listened, sniffed, and motioned Reith to do the same. Reith caught a faint clammy odor, like that of earthworms. In a subdued voice he called down into the hole: "Helsse!" and once again, louder: "Helsse!" To no effect.

They returned to their companions. "It seems that the Pnume play jokes," said Reith in a subdued voice.

They ate a silent breakfast, waited an indecisive fidgeting hour. Then slowly they loaded the boat and departed the island. Reith looked back through the scanscope until the island no longer could be seen.

XI

THE CHANNELS OF THE JINGA CAME TOGETHER; THE SWAMP became a jungle. Fronds and tendrils hung over the black water; giant moths floated like ghosts. The upper strata of the forest was a distinct environment: pink and pale yellow ribbons writhed through the air like eels; black-furred globes with six long white arms swung nimbly from branch to branch. Once, far off along an avenue of vision, Reith saw a cluster of large woven huts high in the branches and a little later the boat passed under a bridge of sticks and coarse ropes. Three naked people came to cross the bridge as the boat drifted close: frail thin-bodied folk with parchment-colored skin. Observing the boat, they halted in shock, then raced across the bridge and disappeared into the foliage.

For a week they sailed and paddled uneventfully, the Jinga growing even wider. One day they passed a canoe from which an old man netted fish; the next day they saw a village on the banks; the day after a power-boat throbbed past. On the night following they halted at a town and spent the night in a riverside inn, standing on stilts over the water.

Two more days they sailed downstream, to a brisk wind from astern. The Jinga was now wide and deep and the wind raised sizable waves. Navigation began to be a problem. Coming to another town they saw a river packet headed downstream; abandoning the boat they took passage for Kabasas on the Parapan.

Three days they rode the packet, enjoying the comfort of hammocks and fresh food. At noon on the fourth day, with the Jinga so broad that the far shore could not be seen, the blue domes of Kabasas appeared on rising land to the west.

Kabasas, like Coad, served as a commercial depot for extensive hinterlands and like Coad seemed to seethe with intrigue. Warehouses and sheds faced the docks; behind, ranks of arched and colonnaded buildings, of beige, gray, white, and dark blue plaster, mounted the hills. A wall of each building, for reasons never clear to Reith, leaned either inward or out, giving the city a curiously irregular appearance, by no means dissonant with the conduct of the inhabitants. These were a slender alert people, with flowing brown hair, wide cheekbones, burning black eyes. The women were notably handsome and Zarfo cautioned all: "If you value your lives, pay no heed to the women! Do not so much as look after them, even though they provoke and tease! They play a strange game here in Kabasas. At any hint of admiration they set up furious outcry and a hundred other women, screaming and cursing rush up to knife the miscreant."

"Hmmf," said Reith. "And the men?"

"They'll save you if they can, and beat the women off, which suits all parties very well. Indeed this is the way of courtship. A man desiring a girl will set upon her and beat her black and blue. No one would think to interfere. If the girl approves, she comes the same way again. When he rushes forth to pummel her, she throws herself on his mercy. Such is the painful wooing of the Kabs."

"It seems somewhat awkward," said Reith.

"Exactly. Awkward and perverse. Such are affairs in Kabasas. During our stay you had best rely on my counsel. First, I nominate the Sea Dragon Inn as a base of operations."

P.W. HAGOPIAN©86

"We'll hardly be here that long. Why not go directly to the dock and find a ship to take us across the Parapan?"

Zarfo pulled at his long black nose. "Things are never so easy. And why cheat ourselves of a sojourn at the Sea Dragon Inn? . . . Perhaps a week or two."

"You naturally intend to pay for your own accommodations?"

Zarfo's white eyebrows dipped sharply. "I am as you know a poor man. My every sequin represents toil. On a joint venture of this sort openhanded generosity should certainly be the rule."

"Tonight," said Reith, "we stay at the Sea Dragon Inn. Tomorrow we leave Kabasas."

Zarfo gave a dismal grunt. "It is not my place to dispute your wishes. Hmmf. As I understand the matter, you plan to arrive at Smargash, recruit a team of technicians, then continue to Ao Hidis?"

"Correct."

"Discretion then! I suggest that we take a ship to Zara across the Parapan and up the Ish River. You have not lost your money?"

"Definitely not."

"Take good care of it. The thieves of Kabasas are deft; they use thongs which reach out thirty feet." Zarfe pointed. "Observe that structure just above the beach? The Sea Dragon Inn!"

The Sea Dragon Inn was indeed a grand establishment, with wide public rooms and pleasant sleeping cubicles. The restaurant was decorated to suggest a submarine garden, even to the dark grottos where members of a local sect, who would not publicly perform the act of deglutition, were served.

Reith ordered fresh linen from the staff haberdashery and descended to the great bath on the low terrace. He scrubbed himself and was sprayed with tonic and massaged with handfuls of fragrant moss. Wrapping himself in a gown of white linen he returned to his chamber.

On the couch sat a man in a soiled dark blue suit. Reith stared. Helsse looked back at him with an unfathomable expression. He made no move and uttered no sound.

The silence was intense.

Reith slowly backed from the room, to stand uncertainly on the balcony, heart pounding as if he had seen a ghost. Zarfo appeared, swaggering back to his room with white hair billowing.

Reith signaled to him. "Come, I want to show you something." He took Zarfo to the door, thrust it ajar, half-expecting to find the room unoccupied. Helsse sat as before. Zarfo whispered: "Is he mad? He sits and stares and mocks us but does not speak."

"Helsse," said Reith. "What are you doing here? What happened to you?"

Helsse rose to his feet. Reith and Zarfo moved involuntarily back. Helsse looked at them with the faintest of smiles. He stepped out on the balcony, walked slowly to the stairs. He turned his head; Reith and Zarfo saw the pale oval of his face; then, like an apparition, he was gone.

"What is the meaning of all this?" Reith asked in a husky voice.

Zarfo shook his head, for once subdued. "The Pnume love their pranks."

"Should we have held him?"

"He could have stayed, had he wished."

"But—I doubt if he is sane."

Zarfo's only response was a hunch-shouldered shrug.

Reith went to the edge of the balcony, looked out over the town. "The Pnume know the very rooms in which we sleep!"

"A person floating down the Jinga ends up at Kabasas," said Zarfo testily. "If he is able, he patronizes the Sea Dragon Inn. This is not an intricate deduction. So much for Pnume omniscience."

* * *

On the following day Zarfo went off by himself and presently returned with a short man with skin the color of mahogany, walking with a sore-footed swagger as if his shoes were too tight. His face was seamed and crooked; small nervous eyes looked slantwise past the beak of his nose. "And here," declared Zarfo grandly, "I give you Sealord Dobagq Hrostilfe, a person of sagacity, who will arrange everything."

Reith thought that he had never seen a more obvious rascal.

"Hrostilfe commands the *Pibar*," explained Zarfo. "For a most reasonable sum he will deliver us to our destination, be it the far coast of Vord."

"How much across the Parapan?" Reith asked.

"Only five thousand sequins, would you believe it?" exclaimed Zarfo.

Reith laughed scornfully. He turned to Zarfo: "I need your help no longer. You and your friend Hrostilfe can try to swindle someone else."

"What?" cried Zarfo. "After I risked my life in that infernal chute and endured all manner of hardship?"

But Reith had walked away. Zarfo came after him, somewhat crestfallen. "Adam Reith, you have made a serious mistake."

Reith nodded grimly. "Instead of an honest man I hired you."

Zarfo swelled up indignantly. "Who dares name me other than honest?"

"I do. Hrostilfe would rent his boat for a hundred sequins. He gave you a price of five hundred. You told him: 'Why should we not both profit? Adam Reith is credulous. I'll name a price and anything over a thousand sequins is mine.' So, be off with you."

Zarfo pulled ruefully at his black nose. "You do me vast wrong. I have only just come from chiding Hrostilfe, who admitted knavery. He now offers his boat at"—Zarfo cleared his throat—"twelve hundred sequins."

"Not a bice more than three hundred."

Zarfo threw his hands in the air and stalked away. Not long after Hrostilfe himself appeared with the plea that Reith inspect his ship. Reith followed him to the *Pibar*: a jaunty craft forty feet long, powered by electrostatic jet. Hrostilfe kept up a half-hectoring, half-plaintive commentary. "A fast seaworthy vessel! Your price is absurd. What of my skills, my sea-lore? Do you appreciate the cost of energy? The voyage will exhaust a power cell: a hundred sequins which I cannot afford. You must pay for energy and additionally for provisions. I am a generous man but I cannot subsidize you."

Reith agreed to pay for energy and a reasonable amount for provisions, but not the installation of new water tanks, extra foul-weather gear, good-luck fetishes for the prow; furthermore he insisted on departure the following day, at which Hrostilfe gave a sour chuckle. "There's one in the eye for the old Lokhar. He had counted on swanking it a week or more at the Sea Dragon."

"He can stay as long as he likes," said Reith, "provided that he pays."

"Small chance of that," chuckled Hrostilfe. "Well then, what about provisions?"

"Buy them. Show me an itemized tally, which I will check in detail."

"I need an advance: a hundred sequins."

"Do you take me for a fool? Remember, tomorrow noon we sail."

"The *Pibar* will be ready," said Hrostilfe in a sullen voice.

Returning to the Sea Dragon Inn, Reith found Anacho on the terrace. Anacho pointed to a black-haired shape leaning against the seawall. "There he stands: Helsse. I called him by name. It was as if he never heard."

Helsse turned his head; his face seemed deathly white. For

a moment or two he watched them, then turned and walked slowly away.

At noon the travelers embarked on the *Pibar*. Hrostilfe gave his passengers a brisk welcome. Reith looked skeptically here and there, wondering in what fashion Hrostilfe thought he had won advantage for himself. "Where are the provisions?"

"In the main saloon."

Reith examined boxes and crates, checked them against Hrostilfe's tally sheet, and was forced to admit that Hrostilfe had secured good merchandise at no great price. But why, he wondered, were they not stored forward in the lazaret? He tried the door, and found it locked.

Interesting, thought Reith. He called Hrostilfe: "Best to stow the stores forward in the lazaret, before we start pitching to the waves."

"All in good time!" declared Hrostilfe. "First things first! Now it's important that we make the most of the morning current!"

"But it will only require a moment. Here, open the door; I will do it myself."

Hrostilfe made a waggish gesture. "I am the most finicky of seamen. Everything must be done just so."

Zarfo, who had come into the saloon, gave the lazaret door a speculative frown. Reith said, "Very well then, just as you like." Zarfo started to speak but catching Reith's gaze, shrugged and held his tongue.

Hrostilfe nimbly hopped here and there, casting off lines, starting the jet, and finally jumping into the control pulpit. The boat surged out to sea.

Reith spoke to Traz, who went to stand behind Hrostilfe. Bringing forth his catapult Traz checked its action, dropped a bolt into the slot, cocked it and hung it loosely at his belt.

Hrostilfe grimaced. "Careful, boy! A foolhardy way to carry your catapult!"

Traz seemed not to hear.

Reith, after a word or two with Zarfo and Anacho, went to the foredeck. Setting fire to some old rags, he held them in the forward ventilator, so that smoke poured down into the lazaret.

Hrostilfe cried out in anger: "What nonsense is this? Are you trying to set us afire?"

Reith set more rags burning and dropped them into the ventilator. From below came a choked cough, then a mutter of voices and a stamping of feet. Hrostilfe jerked his hand toward his pouch, but noticed Traz's intent gaze and his ready catapult.

Reith sauntered aft. Traz said, "His weapon is in his pouch."

Hrostilfe stood rigid with dismay. He made a sudden move but stopped short as Traz jerked up the catapult. Reith detached the pouch, handed it to Traz, took two daggers and a poniard from various parts of Hrostilfe's person. "Go below," said Reith. "Open the door to the lazaret. Instruct your friends to come forth one at a time."

Hrostilfe, gray-faced with fury, hopped below and, after an exchange of threats with Reith, opened the door. Six ruffians came forth, to be disarmed by Anacho and Zarfo and sent up to the deck where Reith thrust them over the side.

The lazaret at last was empty of all but smoke. Hrostilfe was hustled up on deck, where he became unctuous and over-reasonable. "All can be explained! A ridiculous misunderstanding!" But Reith refused to listen and Hrostilfe joined his fellows over the side, where, after shaking his fist and bellowing obscenities at the grinning faces aboard the *Pibar*, he struck out for the shore.

"It appears," said Reith, "that we now lack a navigator. In what direction lies Zara?"

Zarfo's manner was very subdued. He pointed a gnarled black finger. "That should be our heading." He turned to look aft toward the seven bobbing heads. "Incomprehensible to me, the greed of men for money! See to what disasters it leads!'' And Zarfo gave a sanctimonious cluck of the tongue. ''Well then, an unfortunate incident, happily in the past. And now we command the *Pibar*! Ahead: Zara, the Ish River, and Smargash!''

XII

ALL DURING THE FIRST DAY THE PARAPAN WAS SERENE. THE second day was brisk with the *Pibar* pitching up and over a short chop. On the third day a black-brown cloud loomed out of the west, stabbing the sea with lightning. Wind came in massive gusts; for two hours the *Pibar* heaved and tossed; then the storm passed over, and the *Pibar* drove into clement weather.

On the fourth day Kachan loomed ahead. Reith steered the *Pibar* alongside a fishing craft and Zarfo asked the direction of Zara. The fisherman, a swarthy old man with steel rings in his ears, pointed wordlessly. The *Pibar* surged forward, entering the Ish estuary at sunset. The lights of Zara flickered along the western shore, but now, with no reason to put into port, the *Pibar* continued south up the Ish.

The pink moon Az shone on the water; all night the *Pibar* drove. Morning found them in a rich country with rows of stately keel trees along the banks. Then the land began to grow barren, and for a space the river wound through a cluster of obsidian spires. On the next day a band of tall men in black cloaks were seen on the riverbank. Zarfo identified them as Niss tribesmen. They stood motionless, watching the

Pibar surge upstream. ''Give them a wide berth! They live in holes like night-hounds and some say the night-hounds are kinder.''

Late in the afternoon sand dunes closed in upon the river and Zarfo insisted that the *Pibar* be anchored in deep water for the night. ''Ahead are sandbars and shallows. We would be certain to run aground and undoubtedly the Niss have followed. They would grapple the boat and swarm aboard.''

''Won't they attack us if we lay at anchor?''

''No, they fear deep water and never use boats. At anchor we are as safe as if we were already at Smargash.''

The night was clear with both Az and Braz wheeling through the sky of old Tschai. On the riverbank the Niss boldly lit their fires and boiled their pots, and later started up a wild music of fiddles and drums. For hours the travelers sat watching the agile shapes in black cloaks dancing around the fires, kicking, jumping, heads up, heads low; swinging, whirling, prancing with arms akimbo.

In the morning the Niss were nowhere to be seen. The *Pibar* passed through the shallows without incident. Late in the afternoon the travelers came to a village, guarded from the Niss by a line of posts to each of which was chained a skeleton in a rotting black cloak. Zarfo declared the village to be the feasible limit of navigation with Smargash yet three hundred miles south, across a land of deserts, mountain pinnacles and chasms. ''Now we must travel by caravan, over the old Sarsazm Road, to Hamil Zut under the Lokhara Uplands. Tonight I'll make inquiry and learn what's to our advantage.''

Zarfo stayed ashore overnight, returning in the morning with the news that by dint of the most furious bargaining he had exchanged the *Pibar* for first-class passage by caravan to Hamil Zut.

Reith calculated. Three hundred miles? Two hundred sequins a person, at maximum: eight hundred for the four. The *Pibar* was worth ten thousand, even at a sacrifice price. He looked at Zarfo, who ingenuously returned the gaze. ''You will recall,'' said Reith, ''the ill feeling and dissension at Kabasas?''

''Of course,'' declared Zarfo. ''To this day I become anguished by the injustice of your hints.''

''Here is another hint. How much extra did you demand for the *Pibar*—and receive?''

Zarfo gave an uneasy grimace. ''Naturally, I was saving the news to be a glad surprise.''

''How much?''

''Three thousand sequins,'' muttered Zarfo. ''No more, no less. I consider it a fair price up here, far from wealth.''

Reith allowed the figure to pass without challenge. ''Where is the money?''

''It will be paid when we go ashore.''

''And when does the caravan leave?''

''Soon—a day or so. There is a passable inn; we can spend the night ashore.''

''Very well; let us all go now and collect the money.''

Somewhat to Reith's surprise the sack which Zarfo received from the innkeeper contained exactly three thousand sequins, and Zarfo gave a sour sneer and, going into the tavern, called for a pot of ale.

Three days later the caravan started south: a file of twelve power wagons, four mounted with sandblasts. Sarsazm Road led through awesome scenery: gorges and great precipices, the bed of an ancient sea, vistas of distant mountains, sighing forests of keel and blackfern. Occasionally Niss were sighted but they kept their distance and on the evening of the third day the caravan pulled into Hamil Zut, a squalid little town of a hundred mud huts and a dozen taverns.

In the morning Zarfo engaged pack-beasts, equipment and a pair of guides, and the travelers set forth up the trail into the Lokharan highlands.

''This is wild country,'' Zarfo warned them. ''Dangerous beasts are occasionally seen, so be ready with your weapons.''

The trail was steep, the terrain indeed wild. On several occasions they sighted Kar Yan, subtle gray beasts slinking through the rocks, sometimes erect on two legs, sometimes dropping to all six. Another time they encountered a tiger-headed reptile gorging upon a carcass, and were able to pass unmolested.

On the third day after leaving Hamil Zut, the travelers entered Lokhara, a great upland plain; and in the mid-afternoon Smargash appeared ahead. Zarfo now told Reith: "It occurs to me, as it must have to you, that yours is a very ticklish venture."

"Agreed."

"Folk here are not indifferent to the Wankh, and a stranger might easily talk to the wrong people."

"So?"

"It might be better for me to select the personnel."

"Certainly. But leave the question to payment to me."

"As you wish," growled Zarfo.

The countryside was now a prosperous well-watered land, populated by peasant farms. The men, like Zarfo, were tattooed or dyed black, with a mane of white hair. The skins of the women, in contradistinction, were chalky white, and their hair was black. Urchins showed white or black hair according to their sex, but their skins were uniformly the color of the dirt in which they played.

A road ran on a riverbank, under majestic old keels. To either side were small bungalows, each in its bower of vines and shrubs. Zarfo sighed with vast feeling. "Observe me, the transient worker returning to his home. But where is my fortune? How may I buy my cottage by the river? Poverty has forced me to strange ways; I am thrown in with a stone-hearted zealot, who takes his joy thwarting the hopes of a kind old man!"

Reith paid no heed, and presently they entered Smargash.

XIII

REITH SAT IN THE PARLOR OF THE SQUAT CYLINDRICAL COTTAGE he had rented, overlooking the Smargash common, where the young folk spent much time dancing.

Across from him, in wicker chairs, sat five white-haired men of Smargash, a group screened from the twenty Zarfo orginally had approached. The time was middle afternoon; out on the common dancers skipped and kicked to music of concertina, bells and drums.

Reith explained as much of his program as he dared: not a great deal. "You men are here because you can help me in a certain venture. Zarfo Detwiler has informed you that a large sum of money is involved; this is true, even if we fail. If we succeed, and I believe the chances are favorable, you will earn wealth sufficient to satisfy any of you. There is danger, as might be expected, but we shall hold it to a minimum. If anyone does not care to consider such a venture, now is the time to leave."

The oldest of the group, one Jag Jaganig, an expert in the overhaul and installation of control systems, said, "So far we can't say yes or no. None of us would refuse to drag home a sack of sequins, but neither would we care to challenge impossibility for a chancy bice."

"You want more information?" Reith looked from face to face. "This is natural enough. But I don't want to take the merely curious into my confidence. If any of you are definitely not disposed for a dangerous but by no means desperate venture, please identify yourself now."

There was a slight stir of uneasiness but no one spoke out.

Reith waited a moment. "Very well; you must bind yourselves to secrecy."

The group bound themselves by awful Lokhar oaths. Zarfo, plucking a hair from each head, twisted a fiber which he set alight. Each inhaled the smoke. "So are we bound, one to all; if one proves false, the others as one will strike him down."

Reith, impressed by the ritual, had no more qualms about speaking to the point. "I know the exact location of a source of wealth, at a place not on the planet Tschal. We need a spaceship and a crew to operate it. I propose to commandeer a spaceship from the Ao Hidis field; you men shall be the crew. To demonstrate my sanity and good faith, I will pay to each man on the day of departure five thousand sequins. If we try but fail, each man receives another five thousand sequins."

"Each surviving man," grumbled Jag Jaganig.

Reith went on: "If we succeed, ten thousand sequins will seem like ten bice. Essentially, this is the scope of the venture."

The Lokhars shuffled dubiously in their chairs. Jag Jaganig spoke. "We obviously have the basis for an adequate crew here, at least for a Zeno, or a Kud, or even one of the small Kadants. But it is no small matter to so affront the Wankh."

"Or worse, the Wankhmen," muttered Zorofim.

"As I recall," mused Thadzei, "no great vigilance prevailed. The scheme, while startling, seems feasible—provided that the ship we board is in operative condition."

"Aha!" exclaimed Belje. "That 'provided that' is the key to the entire exploit!"

Zarfo jeered: "Naturally there is risk. Do you expect money for nothing?"

"I can hope."

Jag Jaganig inquired: "Assume that the ship is ours. Is further risk entailed?"

"None."

"Who will navigate?"

"I will."

"In what form is this 'wealth'?" demanded Zorofim. "Gems? Sequins? Precious metal? Antiques? Essences?"

"I don't care to go any further into detail, except to guarantee that you will not be disappointed."

The discussion proceeded, with every aspect of the venture subjected to attack and analysis. Alternative proposals were considered, argued, rejected. No one seemed to regard the risk as overwhelming, nor did anyone doubt the group's ability to handle the ship. But none envinced enthusiasm. Jag Jaganig put the situation into focus. "We are puzzled," he told Reith. "We do not understand your purposes. We are skeptical of boundless treasures."

Zarfo said, "Here I must speak. Adam Reith has his faults, which I won't deny. He is stubborn and unwieldy; he is crafty as a zut; he is ruthless when opposed. But he is a man of his word. If he declares a treasure to exist for our taking, that aspect of the matter is closed."

After a moment Belje muttered: "Desperate, desperate! Who wants to learn the truth of the black boxes?"

"Desperate, no," countered Thadzei. "Risky, yes, and may demons run off with the black boxes!"

"I'll take the chance," said Zorofim.

"I as well," said Jag Jaganig. "Who lives forever?"

Belje finally capitulated and declared himself committed. "When shall we leave?"

"As soon as possible," said Reith. "The longer I wait, the more nervous I get."

"And more the chance of someone else running off with

our treasure, hey?'' exclaimed Zarfo. ''That would be a sad case!''

''Give us three days to arrange our affairs,'' said Jag Jaganig.

''And what of the five thousand sequins?'' demanded Thadzei. ''Why not distribute the money now, so that we may have the use of it?''

Reith hesitated no longer than a tenth of a second. ''Since you must trust me, I must trust you.'' He paid to each of the marveling Lokhars fifty purple sequins, worth a hundred white sequins each.

''Excellent!'' declared Jag Jaganig. ''Remember all! Utter discretion! Spies are everywhere. In particular I distrust that peculiar stranger at the inn who dresses like a Yao.''

''What?'' cried Reith. ''A young man, black-haired, very elegant?''

''The person precisely. He stares out over the dancing field with never a word to say.''

Reith, Zarfo, Anacho and Traz went to the inn. In the dim tap rooms sat Helsse, long legs in tight black twill breeches stretched under the heavy table. Brooding, he looked straight ahead and out the doorway to where black-skinned white-haired boys and white-skinned black-haired girls skipped and caracoled in the tawny sunlight.

Reith said: ''Helsse!''

Helsse never shifted his gaze.

Reith came closer. ''Helsse!''

Helsse slowly turned his head; Reith looked into his eyes like lenses of black glass.

''Speak to me,'' urged Reith. ''Helsse! Speak!''

Helsse opened his mouth, uttered a mournful croak. Reith drew back. Helsse watched him incuriously, then returned to his inspection of the dancing field and the dim hills beyond.

Reith joined his comrades to the side where Zarfo poured him a pot of ale. ''What of the Yao? Is he mad?''

"I don't know. He might be feigning. Or under hypnotic control. Or drugged."

Zarfo took a long draft from his pot, wiped the foam from his nose. "The Yao might think it a favor were we to cure him."

"No doubt," said Reith, "but how?"

"Why not call in a Dugbo practitioner?"

"What might that be?"

Zarfo jerked his thumb to the east. "The Dugbo have a camp back of town: shiftless folk in rags and tatters, given to thieving and vice, and musicians to boot. They worship demons, and their practitioners perform miracles."

"So you think the Dugbo can cure Helsse?"

Zarfo drained his pot. "If he is feigning, I assure you he won't feign long."

Reith shrugged. "We have no better occupation for a day or two."

"Exactly my way of thinking," said Zarfo.

The Dugbo practitioner was a spindly little man dressed in brown rags and boots of uncured leather. His eyes were a luminous hazel, his russet hair was confined in three greasy knobs. On his cheek pale cicatrices worked and jumped as he spoke. He did not appear to consider Reith's requirements surprising and with clinical curiosity studied Helsse, who sat sardonically indifferent in one of the wicker chairs.

The practitioner approached Helsse, looked into his eyes, inspected his ears, and nodded as if a suspicion had been verified. He signaled the fat youth who assisted him, then ducking behind Helsse touched him here and there while the youth held a bottle of black essence under Helsse's nose. Helsse presently became passive and relaxed into the chair. The practitioner set heaps of incense alight and fanned the fumes into Helsse's face. Then, while the youth played a nose flute the practitioner sang: secret words, close to Helsse's ears. He put a wad of clay into Helsse's hand; Helsse furiously began to mold the clay and presently set up a mutter.

©
P.W. HAGOPIAN 8

The practitioner signaled to Reith. "A simple case of possession. Notice: the evil flows from the fingers into the clay. Talk to him if you like. Be gentle but command, and he will answer you."

"Helsse," said Reith, "describe your association with Adam Reith."

In a clear voice Helsse spoke. "Adam Reith came to Settra. There had been rumor and speculation, but when he arrived, all was different. By strange chance he came to Blue Jade, my personal vantage, and there I saw him first. Dordolio came after and in his rage maligned Reith as one of the 'cult': a man who fancied himself from the far world Home. I spoke with Adam Reith but learned only confusion. To clarify by acquiescence, third of the Ten Techniques, I took him to the headquarters of the 'cult' and received contradictions. A courier new to Settra followed us. I could not dramatically divert, sixth of the Techniques. Adam Reith killed the courier and took a message of unknown importance; he would not allow me inspection; I could not comfortably insist. I referred him to a Lokhar, again 'clarifying by acquiescence': as it eventuated, the wrong technique. The Lokhar read far into the message. I ordered Reith assassinated. The attempt was bungled. Reith and his band fled south. I received instructions to accompany him and penetrate his motivations. We journeyed east to the Jinga River and downstream by boat. On an island—" Helsse gave a gasping cry and sank back, rigid and trembling.

The practitioner waved smoke into Helsse's face and pinched his nose. "Return to the 'calm' state, and henceforth, when your nose is pinched, return; this shall be an absolute injunction. Now then, answer such questions as are put to you."

Reith asked, "Why do you spy on Adam Reith?"

"I am obligated to do so; furthermore I enjoy such work."

"Why are you obligated?"

"All Wankhmen must serve Destiny."

"Oho. You are a Wankhman?"

"Yes."

And Reith wondered how he could ever have thought otherwise. Tsutso and the Hoch Hars had not been deceived: "Had you been Yao, all would not have gone so well," so had said Tsutso.

Reith glanced ruefully at his comrades, then turned back to Helsse. "Why do the Wankhmen keep spies in Cath?"

"They watch the turn of the 'round'; they guard against a renascence of the 'cult.' "

"Why?"

"It is a matter of stasis. Conditions now are optimum. Any change can only be for the worse."

"You accompanied Adam Reith from Settra to an island in the swamps. What happened there?"

Helsse once more croaked and became catatonic. The practitioner tweaked his nose.

Reith asked. "How did you travel to Kabasas?"

Again Helsse became inert. Reith tweaked his nose. "Tell us why you cannot answer the questions?"

Helsse said nothing. He appeared to be conscious. The practitioner fanned smoke in his face; Reith tweaked his nose and, doing so, saw that Helsse's eyes looked in separate directions. The practitioner rose to his feet, and began to put away his equipment. "That's all. He's dead."

Reith stared from the practitioner to Helsse and back. "Because of the questioning?"

"The smoke permeates the head. Sometimes the subjects live: often, in fact. This one died swiftly; your questions ruptured his sensorium."

The following evening was clear and windy with puffs of dust racing over the vacant dancing field. Through the dusk men in gray cloaks came to the rented cottage. Within, lamps were low and windows shrouded; conversations were conducted in quiet voices. Zarfo spread an old map out on the table, and pointed with a thick black finger. "We can travel to the coast and down, but this is all Niss country. We can fare east around the Sharf to Lake Falas: a long route. Or we can move south, through the Lost Counties, over the Infnets and down to Ao Hidis: the direct and logical route."

Reith asked, "Sky-rafts aren't available?"

Belje, the least enthusiastic of the adventurers, shook his head. "Conditions are no longer as they were when I was a youth. Then you might have selected among half a dozen. Now there are none. Sequins and sky-rafts are both hard to come by. So now, in pursuit of the one, we lack the use of the other."

"How will we travel?"

"To Blalag we ride by power wagon, where perhaps we can hire some sort of conveyance as far as the Infnets. Thereafter, we must go afoot; the old roads south have been destroyed and forgotten."

XIV

FROM SMARGASH TO THE OLD LOKHAR CAPITAL. BLALAG, WAS A three day journey across a windy wasteland. At Blalag the adventurers took shelter at a dingy inn, where they were able to arrange transportation by motor-cart to the mountain-settlement Derduk, far into the Infnets. The journey occupied the better part of two days under uncomfortable conditions. At Derduk the only accommodation was a ramshackle cabin which provoked grumbling among the Lokhars. But the owner, a garrulous old man, stewed a great cauldron of game and wild berries, and the peevishness subsided.

At Derduk the road south became a disused track. At dawn the now somewhat cheerless group of adventurers set forth on foot. All day they traveled through a land of rock pinnacles, fields of rubble and scree. At sundown, with a chill wind sighing through the rocks, they came upon a small black tarn where they passed the night. The next day brought them to the brink of a vast chasm and another day was spent finding a route to the bottom. On the sandy floor beside the river Desidea, on its way east to Lake Falas, the group camped, to be disturbed for much of the night by uncanny hoots and near-human yells, echoing and reechoing through the rocks.

In the morning, rather than attempt the south face of the precipice, they followed the Desidea and presently found a cleft which brought them out upon a high savannah rolling off into the murk.

Two days the adventurers marched south, reaching the extreme ramparts of the Infnets by twilight of the second day, with a tremendous vista across the lands to the south. When night came a sparkle of far lights appeared. "Ao Hidis!" cried the Lokhars in mingled relief and apprehension.

Over the minuscule campfire that night there was much talk of Wankh and Wankhmen. The Lokhars were unanimous in their detestation of the Wankhmen: "Even the Dirdirmen, for all their erudition and preening, are never so jealous of their prerogatives," declared Jag Jaganig.

Anacho gave an airy laugh. "From the Dirdirman point of view Wankhmen are scarcely superior to any of the other sub-races."

"Give the rascals credit," said Zarfo, "they understand the Wankh chimes. I myself am resourceful and perceptive; still, in twenty-five years, I learned only pidgin chords for 'yes,' 'no,' 'stop,' 'go,' 'right,' 'wrong,' 'good,' 'bad.' I must admit to their achievement."

"Bah," muttered Zorofim. "They are born to it; they hear chimes from the first instant of their lives; it is no great achievement."

"One that they make the most of, however," said Belje with something like envy in his voice. "Think; they work at nothing, they have no responsibilities but to stand between the Wankh and the world of Tschai, and they live in refinement and ease."

Reith spoke in a puzzled voice. "A man like Helsse now: he was a Wankhman who lived as a spy. What did he hope to achieve? What Wankh interests did he safeguard in Cath?"

"Wankh interests—none. But remember, the Wankhmen are opposed to change, since any alteration of circumstances can only be to their disadvantage. When a Lokhar begins to understand chimes he is sent away. In Cath—who knows what they fear?'' And Zarfo warmed his hands at the campfire.

The night passed slowly. At dawn Reith looked toward Ao Hidis through his scanscope, but could see little for the mist.

Surly with tension and lack of sleep the group once more set off to the south, keeping to such cover as offered itself.

The city slowly became distinct; Reith located the dock where the *Vargaz* had discharged—how long ago it seemed! He traced the road which led through the market and north past the spacefield. From the heights the city seemed placid, lifeless; the black towers of the Wankhmen brooded over the water. On the spacefield, plain to be seen, were five spaceships.

By noon the party reached the ridge above the city. With great care Reith studied the spacefield, now directly below, through his scanscope. To the left were the repair shops, and nearby a bulk-cargo vessel in a state of obvious disrepair, with scaffolds raised beside exposed machinery. Another ship, this the closest, at the back of the field, seemed to be an abandoned hulk. The condition of the other three vessels was not obvious, but the Lokhars declared them all operable. ''It is a matter of routine,'' said Zorofim. ''When a ship is down for overhaul, it is moved close to the shops. The ships in transit dock yonder, in the 'Load Zone.' ''

''It would seem then that three ships are potentially suitable for our purposes?''

The Lokhars would not go quite so far.

''Sometimes minor repairs are done in the 'Load Zone,' '' said Belje.

''Notice,'' said Thadzei, ''the repair cart by the access ramp. It carries components, cases, and they must come from one of the three ships in the 'Load Zone.' ''

These were two small cargo ships and a passenger vessel. The Lokhars favored the cargo ships, with which they felt familiar. In regard to the passenger vessel, which Reith considered the most suitable, the Lokhars were in disagreement, Zorofim and Thadzei declaring it to be a standard ship in a specialized hull; Jag Jaganig and Belje equally certain that this was either a new design or an elaborate modification, in either case certain to present difficulties.

All day the group studied the spacefield, watching the activity of the workshop and the traffic along the road. During the middle afternoon a black air-car drifted down to land beside the passenger vessel, which now obscured the view, but it appeared that there was a transfer between ship and air-car. Somewhat later Lokhar mechanics brought a case of energy tubes to the ship, which according to Zarfo was a sure signal that the ship was preparing for departure.

The sun sank toward the ocean. The men fell silent, studying the ships which, hardly more than a quarter-mile distant, seemed tantalizingly accessible. Still the question lingered: Which of the three ships in the "Load Zone" offered the maximum opportunity for a successful departure? The consensus favored one of the cargo ships, only Jag Jaganig preferring the passenger ship.

Reith's nerves began to crawl. The next few hours would shape his future, and far too many variables lay beyond his control. Strange that the ships should be guarded so lightly! On the other hand who was apt to attempt the theft of a spaceship? Probably not in the last thousand years had such an act occurred, if ever.

Dusk fell over the landscape; the group began to descend the mountainside. Floodlights illuminated the ground beside the warehouses, the repair shop, the depot in back of the loading zone. The remainder of the field remained in greater or less darkness, the ships casting long shadows away from the lights.

The men scrambled the last few feet down to the base of the hill, crossed a patch of dank marshland, and came to the edge of the field, and here they waited five minutes, watching and listening. The warehouses showed no activity; in the shops a few men still worked.

Reith, Zarfo and Thadzei went forth to reconnoiter. Crouching they ran to the abandoned hulk, where they stood in the shadows.

From the machine shop came the whine of machinery; from the depot a voice called something unintelligible. The three waited ten minutes. In the town at the back of the spacefield long skeins of light had come into being; across the harbor the Wankh towers showed a few glimmers of yellow.

The machine shop became quiet; the workers appeared to be leaving. Reith, Zarfo and Thadzei moved across the field, keeping to the long shadows. They reached the first of the small cargo ships, where again they halted to look and listen: there were no sounds, no alarms. Zarfo and Thadzei went to the entry hatch, heaved it open and entered, while Reith with beating heart stood guard outside.

Ten interminable minutes passed. From within came furtive sounds and once or twice a glimmer of light, which aroused in Reith an intense nervousness.

Finally the two Lokhars returned. "No good," grunted Zarfo. "No air, no energy. Let's try the other."

They stole quickly across the bands of light and shadow to the second cargo ship; as before Zarfo and Thadzei entered while Reith stood at the port. The Lokhars returned almost immediately. "Under repair," Zarfo reported glumly. "This is where the component cases came from."

They turned to look at the passenger vessel. "It's not a standard design," Zarfo grumbled. "Still, the instruments and layout may be familiar to us."

"Let's go aboard and look," said Reith. But now a light flared across the field. Reith's first thought was that they had been discovered. But the light played toward the passenger vessel. From the direction of the gate came a low easy-moving shape. The vehicle stopped beside the passenger vessel; a number of dark figures alighted—how many could not be ascertained in the glare. With a curiously abrupt and heavy motion, the figures entered the ship.

"Wankh," muttered Zarfo. "They're going aboard."

"It would mean that the ship is ready for departure," said Reith. "A chance we can't afford to miss!"

Zarfo demurred. "It's one thing to steal an empty ship, another coping with a half a dozen Wankh, and Wankhmen as well."

"How do you know Wankhmen are aboard?"

"Because of the lights. Wankh project pulses of radiation and observe the reflections."

Behind them came a faint sound. Reith whirled to find Traz. "We became worried; you were gone so long."

"Go back; bring everyone here. If we have the opportunity, we'll board the passenger ship. It's the only one available."

Traz vanished into the darkness. Five minutes later the entire group stood in the shadow of the cargo ship.

Half an hour went by. In the passenger ship shapes moved across the lights, performing activities beyond the comprehension of the nervous men. In husky whispers they debated possible courses of action. Should they try to storm the ship now? Almost certainly departure was in the offing. Such action was obviously reckless. The group decided to pursue a conservative course and return into the mountains to await a more propitious occasion. As they started back, a number of Wankh issued from the vessel and lurched to the vehicle, which almost immediately left the field. Within the ship lights still glowed. No further activity was evident.

"I'm going to give it a look," said Reith. He ran across the field, followed by the others. They mounted the ramp, passed through an embarkation port into the ship's main saloon, which was unoccupied. "Everybody to his station," said Reith. "Let's take it up!"

"If we can," grumbled Zorofim.

Traz cried out a warning; turning, Reith saw that a single Wankh had entered the saloon, watching in nonplussed disapproval. It was a black creature somewhat larger than a man, with a heavy torso, a squat head from which two black lenses flickered at half-second intervals. The legs were short; the feet were splayed webs; it carried no weapons or implements; in fact wore no garment or harness of any sort. From a sound organ at the base of the skull came four reverberating chimes, which, considering the circumstances, seemed measured and unexcited. Reith stepped forward, pointed to a settee, to indicate that it should sit down. The Wankh stood motionless, looking after the Lokhars who had gone their various ways, checking engines, energy, supplies, oxygen. The Wankh at last seemed to understand the events which were taking place. It took a step toward the exit port, but Reith barred the way and once again pointed to the settee. The Wankh loomed in front of him, the glassy eyes flickering. Once again the chimes sounded, more peremptory than before.

Zarfo returned to the saloon. "The ship is in order. But it's an unfamiliar model, as I feared."

"Can we take it up?"

"We'll have to make sure we know what we are doing. It may be minutes or hours."

"Then we can't let the Wankh go."

"Awkward," said Zarfo.

The Wankh thrust forward; Reith pushed it back and displayed his hand gun. The Wankh uttered a loud chime. Zarfo made a chirping sound. The Wankh drew back.

Reith asked: "What did you say?"

"I just gave the pidgin sound for 'danger.' It seems to understand well enough."

"I wish it would sit down; it makes me nervous standing there."

"Wankh almost never sit," said Zarfo and went to seal the entrance port.

Time passed. From various locations about the ship came calls and exclamations from the Lokhars. At Reith's direction, Traz stood in the observation dome, watching over the field. The Wankh stood stolidly, apparently at a loss for action.

P.W. HAGOPIAN©'86

The ship shuddered; the lights flickered, went dim, came on bright once more. Zarfo looked into the saloon. "We've got the engines pumping. Now if Thadzei can figure out the control configurations—"

Traz called down: "The car is coming back. The floodlight has just gone on, to light the field."

Thadzei ran through the saloon, jumped up to the control console. He peered this way and that, while Zarfo stood by his side urging him to haste. Reith set Anacho to guarding the Wankh, joined Traz in the observation dome. The car was slowing to a stop beside the ship.

Zarfo pointed here and there across the control panel; Thadzei nodded doubtfully, thrust at a set of pressure pads. The ship shuddered and heaved; Reith felt acceleration underfoot. He was departing Tschai! Thadzei made adjustments; the ship pitched. Reith reached for a stanchion; the Wankh stumbled and fell upon the settee, where it remained. From elsewhere about the ship came full-throated Lokhar curses.

Reith made his way to the bridge, to stand beside Thadzei, who desperately worked the controls, testing first one pad, then another. Reith asked: "Is there an automatic pilot?"

"Bound to be, somewhere. I can't locate the engagement. These are by no means standard controls."

"Do you know what you are doing?"

"No."

Reith looked down at the dark face of Tschai. "So long as we are going up and not down, we're in good shape."

"If I had an hour, a single hour," moaned Thadzei, "I could trace out the circuits."

Jag Jaganig came into the saloon to make a querulous protest. Thadzei called back: "I'm doing the best I can!"

"It's not good enough! We'll crash!"

"Not yet," said Thadzei grimly. "I see a lever I haven't tried." He pulled the lever; the ship skidded alarmingly and thrust off at great speed to the east. Once more the Lokhars gave a series of anguished cries. Thadzei moved the lever back to its original position. The ship came to a trembling stasis. Thadzei gave a great tremulous sigh, peering back and forth across the panel. "Like none I have ever seen!"

Reith looked out the port but saw nothing but darkness. Zarfo spoke in a calm voice: "Our altitude is not quite a thousand feet. . . . Now it is nine hundred. . . ."

Thadzei desperately worked the controls. Once again the ship lurched and fled eastward. "Up, up!" screamed Zarfo. "We're diving into the ground!"

Thadzei brought the ship back to a halt."Well then, this toggle will surely activate the repulsors." He gave it a twitch. From aft came a sinister crackle, a muffled explosion. The Lokhars yelled mournfully. Zarfo read the altimeter. "Five hundred . . . Four hundred . . . Three . . . Two . . . One . . ."

Contact: a splash, a bobbing and pitching, then silence. The ship was afloat, apparently undamaged, in an unknown body of water. The Parapan? The Schanizade? Reith threw up his hands in fatalistic despair. Back once more to Tschai.

Reith jumped down to the saloon. The Wankh stood like a statue. Whatever its emotions, none were evident.

Reith went aft to the engine room, where Jag Jaganig and Belje looked disconsolately at a smoldering panel. "An overload," said Belje. "Circuits and nodes are certainly melted."

"Can we make repairs?"

Belje made a glum sound. "If tools and parts are aboard."

"If time is given to us," said Jag Jaganig.

Reith returned to the saloon. He threw himself down upon a settee and stared bleakly at the Wankh. The plan had succeeded . . . almost. He leaned back, sodden with fatigue. The others must be feeling the same. No useful purpose could be served by going longer without rest. He got to his feet, called the group together. Two-man watches were set; the others slumped upon settees to sleep as best they might.

The night passed. Az raced across the sky, followed by Braz. Dawn revealed a placid expanse which Zarfo indentified as Lake Falas. "And never has it served a more useful purpose!"

Reith went out on the top surface of the hull and searched the horizons through his scanscope. Hazy water stretched to south, east and west. To the north was a low shore toward which the ship was drifting, propelled by a gentle breeze from the south. Reith went back into the ship. The Lokhars had detached a panel and were unenthusiastically discussing the damage. Their attitudes gave Reith all the information he needed.

In the saloon he found Anacho and Traz gnawing on spheres of black paste encased in a hard white rind which they had taken from a locker. Reith offered one of the spheres to the Wankh, who paid no heed. Reith ate the sphere himself, finding it similar to cheese. Zarfo presently joined him and verified what Reith already had guessed. "Repairs are not feasible. A whole bank of crystals is destroyed. There are no spares aboard."

Reith gave a gloomy nod. "As I expected."

"What next?" demanded Zarfo.

"As soon as the wind blows us ashore we disembark and return to Ao Hidis for another try."

Zarfo grunted. "What of the Wankh?"

"We'll have to let him go his own way. I certainly don't plan to murder him."

"A mistake," sniffed Anacho. "Best kill the repulsive beast."

"For your information," said Zarfo, "the main Wankh citadel Ao Khaha is situated on Lake Falas. It will not be far distant."

Reith went back out on the foredeck. The first tussocks of the shore were only half a mile distant; beyond lay quagmire. To ground at the edge of such a morass would be highly inconvenient, and Reith was glad to see that the wind, shifting to the east, seemed to be moving the ship slowly to the west, perhaps aided by a sluggish current. Turning the scanscope along the shore Reith was able to distinguish a set of irregular juts and promontories far to the west.

From within came the sound of expostulation, followed by the thud of heavy footsteps. Out on the foredeck came the Wankh, followed by Anacho and Traz. The Wankh fixed Reith for half a second with its flicking vision, long enough to register an image, then turned by slow degrees to look around the horizon. Before Reith could prevent it—even were he able to do so—the Wankh stepped forward, ran with its peculiar lurching gait down the side of the ship and plunged into the water. Reith caught a glimpse of wet black hide, then the creature was gone into the depths.

Reith searched the surface for a period but saw no more of the Wankh. An hour later, checking the progress of the vessel, he once more turned the scanscope on the western shore. To his cold dismay he saw that the shapes he had thought to be crags were the black glass towers of an extensive Wankh fortress city. Wordlessly Reith examined the swamp to the north with a new interest born of desperation.

Tussocks of white grass protruded like hairy wens from fields of black slime and stagnant ponds. Reith went below to seek material for a raft, but found nothing. The padding of the settee was welded to the structure and came away in shreds and chunks. There was no lifeboat aboard. Reith returned to the deck and wondered what his next move should be. The Lokhars joined him: disconsolate figures in wheat-colored smocks, wind blowing the white hair back from their craggy black faces.

Reith spoke to Zarfo: "Do you know the place yonder?"

"It must be Ao Khaha."

"If we are taken, what can we expect?"

"Death."

The morning passed; the sun climbing toward noon dissolved the haze which shrouded the horizons, and the towers of Ao Khaha stood distinct.

The ship was noted. On the water under the city appeared a barge, which surged across the water leaving a ribbon of white wake. Reith studied it through the scanscope. Wankhmen stood on the deck, perhaps a dozen, curiously alike: slender men with death-pale skins, saturnine or, in some instances, ascetic features. Reith considered resistance: perhaps a desperate attempt to seize the barge? He decided against such a trial, which almost certainly could not succeed.

The Wankhmen scrambled aboard the ship. Ignoring Reith, Traz and Anacho, they addressed the Lokhars. "All down to the barge. Do you carry weapons?"

"No," grunted Zarfo.

"Quick then." Now they noticed Anacho. "What is this? A Dirdirman?" And they gave chuckles of soft surprise. They inspected Reith. "And what sort is that one?" "A motley crew, to be sure!" "Now then, all down to the barge!"

The Lokhars went first, hulk-shouldered, knowing what lay ahead. Reith, Traz and Anacho followed.

"All! Stand on the deck, at the gunwales, in a neat line. Turn your backs." And the Wankhmen brought out their hand guns.

The Lokhars started to obey. Reith had not expected such casual and perfunctory slaughter. Furious that he had not resisted from the first he cried out: "Should we let them kill us so easily? Let's make a fight of it!"

The Wankhmen gave sharp orders: "Unless you wish worse, quick! To the gunwales!"

Near the barge the water roiled. A black shape floated lazily to the surface and produced four plangent chimes. The Wankhmen stiffened; their faces sagged into sneers of annoyance. They waved at their captives. "Back then, into the cockpit."

The barge returned to the great black fortress, the Wankhmen muttering among themselves. It passed behind a breakwater, magnetically clamped itself to a pier. The prisoners were marshaled ashore and through a portal, into Ao Khaha.

XV

SURFACES OF BLACK GLASS, STARK WALLS AND AREAS OF BLACK concrete, angles, blocks, masses: a negation of organic shape. Reith wondered at the architecture; it seemed remarkably abstract and severe. Into a cul-de-sac, walled on three sides with dark concrete, the captives were taken. "Halt! Remain in place!" came the command.

The prisoners, with no choice, halted and stood in a surly line.

"Water yourselves at that spigot. Perform evacuation into that trough. Make no noise or disturbance." The Wankhmen departed, leaving the prisoners unguarded.

Reith said in a wondering voice, "We haven't even been searched! I still have my weapons."

"It's not far to the portal," said Traz. "Why should we wait here to be killed?"

"We'd never reach the portal," growled Zarfo.

"So we must stand here like docile animals?"

"That's what I plan to do," said Belje, with a bitter glance toward Reith. "I'll never see Smargash more, but I may escape with my life."

Zorofim gave a rude laugh. "In the mines?"

"I know only rumor of the mines."

"Once a man goes underground he never emerges. There are ambushes and terrible tricks by Pnume and Pnumekin. If we are not executed out of hand we will go to the mines."

"All for avarice and mad folly!" lamented Belje. "Adam Reith, you have much to answer for!"

"Quiet, poltroon," said Zarfo without heat. "No one forced you to come. The fault is our own. We should abase ourselves before Reith; he trusted our knowledge; we showed him ineptitude."

"All of us did our best," said Reith. "The operation was risky; we failed; it's as simple as that . . . As for trying to escape from here—I can't believe that they'd leave us alone, unguarded, free to walk away."

Jag Jaganig snorted sadly. "Don't be too sure; to the Wankhmen we are animals."

Reith turned to Traz, whose perceptions at times bewildered him. "Could you find your way to the portal?"

"I don't know. Not directly. There were many turns. The buildings confuse me."

"Then we had best remain here. . . . There's a bare chance that we can talk our way out of the situation."

The afternoon passed, then the long night, with Az and Braz creating fantasies of shapes and shadows. In the chill morning, cantankerous with stiff joints and hunger, and increasingly restless because of their captors' inattention, even the most fearful of the Lokhars were peering out of the cul-de-sac and speculating as to the whereabouts of the portal through the black glass wall.

Reith still counseled patience. "We'd never make it. Our only hope as I see it is that the Wankh may decide to be lenient with us."

"Why should they be lenient?" sneered Thadzei. "Their justice is forthright: the same justice we use toward pests."

Jag Jaganig was no less pessimistic. "We will never see

the Wankh. Why else do they maintain the Wankhmen, except to stand between themselves and Tschai?"

"We shall see," said Reith.

The morning passed. The Lokhars slumped torpidly against a wall. Traz, as usual, maintained his equanimity. Contemplating the boy, Reith could not hep but wonder as to the source of his fortitude. Innate character? Fatalism? Did the personality of Onmale, the emblem he had worn so long, still shape his soul?

But other problems were more immediate. "This delay can't be accidental," Reith fretted to Anacho. "There must be a reason. Are they trying to demoralize us?"

Anacho, as peevish as any of the others, said, "There are better ways than this."

"Are they waiting for something to happen? What?"

Anacho could supply no answers.

Late in the afternoon three Wankhmen appeared. One of these, wearing thin silver greaves and a silver medallion on a chain around his neck, appeared to be a person of importance. He surveyed the group with eyebrows lofted in mingled disapproval and amusement, as if at naughty children. "Well then," he said briskly, "which among you is the leader of this group?"

Reith came forward with as much dignity as he could summon. "I am."

"You? Not one of the Lokhars? What did you hope to achieve?"

"May I ask who adjudicates our offense?" Reith asked.

The Wankhman was taken aback. " 'Adjudication?' What needs to be adjudicated? The only point at issue, and a minor one, is your motive."

"I can't agree with you," said Reith in a reasonable voice. "Our transgression was a simple theft; only by sheer accident did we take aloft a Wankh."

"A Wankh! Do you realize his identity? No, of course not. He is a savant of the highest level, an Original Master."

"And he wants to know why we took his spaceship?"

"What then? It is no concern of yours. You need only transmit the information on through me; that is my function."

"I'll be glad to do so, in his presence, and, I hope, in surroundings more appropriate than a back alley."

"*Zff*, but you are a cool one. Do you answer to the name of Adam Reith?"

"I am Adam Reith."

"And you recently visited Settra in Cath, where you associated with the so-called 'Yearning Refluxives'?"

"Your information is at fault."

"Be that as it may, we want your reason for stealing a spaceship."

"Be on hand when I communicate with the Original Master. The matter is complex and I am certain he will have questions which cannot be answered casually."

The Wankhman swung away in disgust.

Zarfo muttered, "You are a cool one indeed! But what do you gain by talking to the Wankh?"

"I don't know. It's worth trying. I suspect that the Wankhmen report only as much as suits their purposes."

"That's understood by everyone but the Wankh."

"How can it be? Are they innocent? Or remote?"

"Neither. They have no other sources of information. The Wankhmen make sure the situation remains that way. The Wankh have small interest in the affairs of Tschai; they're only here to counter the Dirdir threat."

"Bah," said Anacho. "The 'Dirdir threat' is a myth; the Expansionists are gone thusands of years."

"Then why are they still feared by the Wankh?" demanded Zarfo.

"Mutual distrust; what else?"

"Natural antipathy. The Dirdir are an insufferable race."

Anacho walked away in a huff. Zarfo laughed. Reith shook his head in mild disapproval.

Zarfo now said, "Take my advice, Adam Reith: don't

antagonize the Wankhmen, because you can't win but through them. Ingratiate, truckle, fawn—and at least they'll bear you no malice."

"I'm not too proud to truckle," said Reith, "if it would do any good—which it won't. Our only hope is to push ahead. . . . And I've come up with an idea or two which may help our case, if we get a chance to talk with the Wankh."

"You won't defeat the Wankhmen that way," gloomed Zarfo. "They'll tell the Wankh only as much as they see fit, and you'll never know the difference."

"What I'd like to do," said Reith, "is work up to a situation where only the truth makes sense and where every other statement is an obvious falsity."

Zarfo shook his head in puzzlement and walked to the spigot to drink. Reith remembered that none of the group had eaten for almost two days; small wonder they were listless and irritable.

Three Wankhmen appeared. The official who previously had spoken to Reith was not among them. "Come along. Look sharp, now; form a neat line."

"Where are we going?" Reith asked, but received no reply.

The group walked five minutes, through odd-angled streets and irregular courts, by acute and obtuse angles, past unexpected juts and occasional clear vistas, through deep shadow and the wan shine of Carina 4269. They entered the ground floor of a tower, entered an elevator which took them up a hundred feet and opened upon a large octagonal hall.

The chamber was dim; a great lenticular bulge in the roof held water; windblown ripples modulated light from the sky and sent it dancing around the hall. Tremors of sound were barely audible, sighing chords, complex disonances; sound both more and less than music. The walls were stained and discolored, a fact which Reith found peculiar, until looking closer he recognized Wankh ideograms, immense and intricately detailed, one to each wall. Each ideogram, thought Reith, represented a chime; each chime was the sonic equivalent of a visual image. Here, reflected Reith, were highly abstract pictures.

The chamber was empty. The group waited in silence while the almost unheard chords drifted in and out of consciousness, and amber sunlight, refracted and broken into shimmers, swam through the room.

Reith heard Traz gasp in surprise: a rare event. He turned. Traz pointed. "Look yonder!"

Standing in an alcove was Helsse, head bent in an attitude of brooding reverie. His guise was new and strange. He wore black Wankhman garments; his hair was close-cropped; he looked a person worlds apart from the suave young man Reith had encountered in Blue Jade Palace. Reith looked at Zarfo. "You told me he was dead!"

"So he seemed to me! We put him out in the corpse shed, and in the morning he was gone. We thought the night-hounds had come for him."

Reith called: "Helsse! Over here! It's Adam Reith!"

Helsse turned his head, looked at him and Reith wondered how he ever could have taken Helsse for anything but a Wankhman. Helsse came slowly across the chamber, a half-smile on his face. "So here: the sorry outcome to our exploits."

"The situation is discouraging," Reith agreed. "Can you help us?"

Helsse raised his eyebrows. "Why should I? I find you personally offensive, without humility or ease. You have subjected me to a hundred indignities; your pro-'cult' bias is repulsive; the theft of a space vessel with an Original aboard makes your request absurd."

Reith considered him a moment. "May I ask why you are here?"

"Certainly. To supply information in regard to you and your activities."

Reith mulled the matter over. "Are we so important?"

"So it would seem," said Helsse indifferently.

Four Wankh entered the chamber, and stood by the far wall: four massive black shadwos. Helsse stood straighter; the other Wankhmen became silent. It was apparent, thought Reith, that whatever the total attitude of the Wankhmen toward the Wankh might be, that attitude included a great deal of respect.

The prisoners were urged forward, and ranged in a line before the Wankh. A minute passed, during which nothing happened. Then the Wankh exchanged chimes: soft muffled sounds at half-second intervals, apparently unintelligible to the Wankhmen. Another silence ensued, then the Wankh addressed the Wankhmen, producing triads of three quick notes, like xylophone trills, in what seemed to be a simplified or elemental usage.

The oldest Wankhman stepped forward, listened, turned to the prisoners. "Which of you is the pirate-master?"

"None of us," said Reith. "We are not pirates."

One of the Wankh uttered interrogatory chimes. Reith thought he recognized the Original Master. The Wankhmen, somewhat grudgingly, brought forth a small keyed instrument which he manipulated with astonishing deftness.

"Tell him further," said Reith, "that we regret the inconvenience we caused him. Circumstances compelled us to take him aloft."

"You are not here to argue," said the Wankhman, "but to render information, after which the usual processes will occur."

Again the Master uttered chimes and was answered. Reith asked: "What is he saying, and what did you tell him?"

The senior Wankhman said, "Speak only when you are directly addressed."

Helsse came forward and, producing his own instrument, played chimes at length. Reith began to feel uneasy and frustrated. Events were ranging far beyond his control. "What is Helsse saying?"

"Silence."

''At least inform the Wankh that we have a case which we want to present.''

''You will be notified if it becomes necessary for you to testify. The hearing is almost at an end.''

''But we haven't had a chance to speak!''

''Silence! Your persistence is offensive!''

Reith turned to Zarfo. ''Tell the Wankh something! Anything!''

Zarfo blew out his cheeks. Pointing at the Wankhmen he made chirping sounds. The senior Wankhman said sternly: ''Quiet, you are interrupting.''

''What did you tell him?'' asked Reith.

''I said 'Wrong, wrong, wrong,' That's all I know.''

The Master spoke chimes, indicating Reith and Zarfo. The senior Wankhman, visibly exasperated, said: ''The Wankh want to know where you planned to commit your piracies, or, rather, where you planned to take the spaceship.''

''You are not translating correctly,'' protested Reith. ''Did you tell him that we are not pirates?''

Zarfo again made sounds for ''Wrong, wrong, wrong!''

The Wankhman said, ''You are obviously pirates, or lunatics.'' Turning back to the Wankh, he played his instrument, misrepesenting, so Reith was sure, what had been said. Reith turned to Helsse. ''What is he telling them? That we are not pirates?''

Helsse ignored him.

Zarfo guffawed, to everyone's astonishment. He muttered in Reith's ear: ''Remember the Dugbo? Pinch Helsse's nose.''

Reith said, ''Helsse.''

Helsse turned him an austere gaze. Reith stepped forward, tweaked his nose. Helsse seemed to become rigid. ''Tell the Wankh that I am a man of Earth, the world of human origin,'' said Reith, ''that I took the spaceship only in order to return home.''

Helsse woodenly played a set of trills and runs. The other Wankhmen became instantly agitated—sufficient proof that

Helsse had translated accurately. They began to protest, to press forward, to drown out Helsse's chimes, only to be brought up short by a great belling sound from the Master.

Helsse continued, and at last came to an end.

"Tell them further," said Reith, "that the Wankhmen falsified my remarks, that they consistently do so to further their private purposes."

Helsse played. The other Wankhmen again started a great protest, and again were rebuked.

Reith warmed to his task. He voiced one of his surmises, striking boldly into the unknown: "Tell them that the Wankhmen destroyed my spaceship, killing all aboard except myself. Tell them that our mission was innocent, that we came investigating radio signals broadcast a hundred and fifty Tschai-years ago. At this time the Wankhmen destroyed the cities Settra and Ballisidre from which the signals emanated, with great loss of life, and all for the same reason: to prevent a new situation which might disturb the Wankh-Dirdir stalemate."

The instant uproar among the Wankhmen convinced Reith that his accusations had struck home. Again they were silenced. Helsse played the instrument with the air of a man astounded by his own actions.

"Tell them," said Reith, "that the Wankhmen have systematically distorted truth. They undoubtedly have prolonged the Dirdir war. Remember, if the war ended, the Wankh would return to their home world, and the Wankhmen would be thrown upon their own resources."

Helsse, gray-faced, struggled to drop the instrument, but his fingers refused to do his bidding. He played. The other Wankhmen stood in dead silence. This was the most telling accusation of all. The senior Wankhman shouted: "The interview is at an end! Prisoners, form your line! March!"

Reith told Helsse: "Request that the Wankh order all the other Wankhmen to depart, so that we may communicate without interruption."

Helsse's face twitched; sweat poured down his face.

"Translate my message," said Reith.

Helsse obeyed.

Silence held the chamber, with the Wankhmen gazing in apprehension toward the Wankh.

The Master uttered two chimes.

The Wankhmen muttered among themselves. They came to a terrible decision. Out came their weapons; they turned them, not upon the prisoners, but upon the four Wankh. Reith and Traz sprang forward, followed by the Lokhars. The weapons were wrested away.

The Master uttered two quiet chimes.

Helsse listened, then slowly turned to Reith. "He commands that you give me the weapon you hold."

Reith relinquished the gun. Helsse turned toward the other three Wankhmen, pushed the trigger-button. The three fell dead, their heads shattered.

The Wankh stood a moment in silence, assessing the situation. Then they departed the hall. The erstwhile prisoners remained with Helsse and the corpses. Reith took the gun from Helsse's cold fingers, before he thought to use it again.

The chamber began to grow murky with the coming of dusk. Reith studied Helsse, wondering how long the hypnotic state would persist. He said, "Take us outside the walls."

"Come."

Through the black and gray city Helsse took the group, finally to a small steel door. Helsse touched a latch; the door swung aside. Beyond, a spine of rock led through the dusk to the mainland.

The group filed through the gap into the open air. Reith turned to Helsse. "Ten minutes after I touch your shoulder, resume your normal condition. You will remember nothing of what has happened during the last hour. Do you understand?"

"Yes."

Reith touched Helsse's shoulder; the group hurried away through the twilight. Before a jut of rock hid them from sight Reith looked back. Helsse stood where they had left him, looking somewhat wistfully after them.

XVI

IN A PATCH OF ROUGH FORESTLAND THE GROUP SLUMPED DOWN in total fatigue, their stomachs crawling with hunger. By the light of the two moons Traz searched through the undergrowth and found a clump of pilgrim plant, and the group made their first meal in two days. Somewhat refreshed, they moved on through the night, up a long slope. At the top of the ridge, they turned to look back, toward the gloomy silhouette of Ao Khaha on the moonlit sky. For a few minutes they stood, each man thinking his own thoughts, then they continued north.

In the morning over a breakfast of toasted fungus, Reith opened his pouch. "The expedition has been a failure. As I promised, each man receives another five thousand sequins. Take them now, with my gratitude for your loyalty."

Zarfo took the purple-glowing pellets gingerly, weighed them in his fingers. "Above all I am an honest man, and since this was the structure of the contract, I will accept the money."

Jag Jaganig said: "Let me ask you a question, Adam Reith. You told the Wankh that you were a man from a far world, the home of man. Is this correct?"

"It is what I told the Wankh."

"You are such a man, from such a planet?"

"Yes. Even though Anacho the Dirdirman makes a wry face."

"Tell us something of this planet."

Reith spoke for an hour, while his comrades sat staring into the fire.

Anacho at last cleared his throat. "I do not doubt your sincerity. But, as you say, the history of Earth is short compared to the history of Tschai. It is obvious that far in the past the Dirdir visited Earth and left a colony from which all Earthmen are descended."

"I could prove otherwise," said Reith, "if our venture had been successful and we had all journeyed to Earth."

Anacho poked the fire with a stick. "Interesting. . . . The Dirdir of course would not sell or transfer a spaceship. Such a theft as we perpetrated upon the Wankh would be impossible. Still—at the Great Sivish Spaceyards almost any component can be acquired, by purchase or discreet arrangement. One only needs sequins—a considerable sum, true."

"How much?" asked Reith.

"A hundred thousand sequins would work wonders."

"No doubt. At the moment I have barely the hundredth part of that."

Zarfo threw over his five thousand sequins. "Here. It pains me like the loss of a leg. But let these be the first coins in the pot."

Reith returned the money. "At the moment they would only make a forlorn rattling sound."

Thirteen days later the group came down out of the Infnets to Blalag, where they boarded a power wagon and so returned to Smargash.

For three days Reith, Anacho and Traz ate, slept and watched the young folk at their dancing.

On the evening of the third day Zarfo joined them in the

tap-room. "All look sleek and lazy. Have you heard the news?"

"What news?"

"First, I have acquired a delightful property on a bend of the Whisfer River, with five fine keels, three psillas and an asponistra, not to mention the tayberries. Here I shall end my days—unless you tempt me forth on another mad venture. Secondly, two technicians this morning returned to Smargash from Ao Hidis. Vast changes are in the wind! The Wankhmen are departing the fortresses; they have been driven out and now live in huts with the Blacks and Purples. It appears that the Wankh will no longer tolerate their presence."

Reith chuckled. "At Dadiche we found an alien race exploiting men. At Ao Hidis we found men exploiting an alien race. Both conditions are now changed. Anacho, would you care to be liberated from your enervating philosophy and become a sane man?"

"I want demonstration, not words. Take me to Earth."

"We can hardly walk there."

"At the Great Sivish Spaceyards are a dozen spaceboats, needing only procurement and assembly."

"Yes, but where are the sequins?"

"I don't know," said Anacho.

"Nor I," said Traz.

BLUEJAY ILLUSTRATED EDITIONS

Each Bluejay Illustrated Edition is an outstanding work of imaginative literature, complemented by interior illustrations created especially for the book by a great artist working in the science fiction or fantasy field. All Bluejay Illustrated Editions are printed on acid-free paper in a handsome trade paperback format.

Following is a complete list of volumes already published in this distinguished series:

1: *Too Long A Sacrifice* by Mildred Downey Broxon
Illustrated by Judith Mitchell $7.95

2: *Riding the Torch* by Norman Spinrad
Illustrated by Tom Kidd $6.95

3: *Venus Plus X* by Theodore Sturgeon
Illustrated by Rowena Morrill $7.95

4: *Darker Than You Think* by Jack Williamson
Illustrated by David G. Klein $7.95

5: *True Names* by Vernor Vinge
Illustrated by Bob Walters $6.95

6: *Earthblood* by Keith Laumer and Rosel George Brown
Illustrated by Alan Gutierrez $8.95

7: *The Dreaming Jewels* by Theodore Sturgeon
Illustrated by Rowena Morrill $7.95

8: *Land of Unreason* by L. Sprague de Camp and Fletcher Pratt
Illustrated by Tim Kirk $7.95

9: *Rogue Queen* by L. Sprague de Camp
Illustrated by Philip Hagopian $7.95

10: *The Legion of Time* by Jack Williamson
Illustrated by Ilene Meyer $8.95

11: *Chasch (Tschai I)* The Planet of Adventure tetralogy by Jack Vance
Illustrated by Philip Hagopian $8.95

12: *Sherlock Holmes Through Time and Space* edited by Isaac Asimov, Martin Harry Greenberg and Charles G. Waugh
Illustrated by Tom Kidd and Richard Berry $8.95

13: *The Witling* by Vernor Vinge
Illustrated by Doug Beekman $8.95

14: *Wankh (Tschai II)* The Planet of Adventure tetralogy by Jack Vance.
Illustrated by Philip Hagopian. $8.95

To purchase copies of any Bluejay books, send a check for the retail price of the book plus $1.50 for postage and handling and 25¢ for each additional book to:

Cash Sales
St. Martin's Press, Inc.
175 Fifth Avenue
New York, NY 10010

All checks must be made out to St. Martin's Press, Inc.

BECOME A BLUEJAY WATCHER

If you enjoyed this book and would like to know about some of the nearly one hundred Bluejay Books, write to us for a free list of books, c/o Dept. CATALOG.